Vilonia Beebe TAKES CHARGE

Kristin L. Gray

A Paula Wiseman Book

Simon & Schuster Books for Young Readers

NEW YORK   LONDON   TORONTO   SYDNEY   NEW DELHI

SIMON & SCHUSTER BOOKS FOR YOUNG READERS

An imprint of Simon & Schuster Children's Publishing Division

1230 Avenue of the Americas, New York, New York 10020

This book is a work of fiction. Any references to historical events, real people, or real places are used fictitiously. Other names, characters, places, and events are products of the author's imagination, and any resemblance to actual events or places or persons, living or dead, is entirely coincidental.

Text copyright © 2017 by Kristin L. Gray

Cover illustrations copyright © 2017 by Emma Trithart

All rights reserved, including the right of reproduction in whole or in part in any form.

SIMON & SCHUSTER BOOKS FOR YOUNG READERS

is a trademark of Simon & Schuster, Inc.

For information about special discounts for bulk purchases, please contact Simon & Schuster Special Sales at 1-866-506-1949 or business@simonandschuster.com.

The Simon & Schuster Speakers Bureau can bring authors to your live event. For more information or to book an event, contact the Simon & Schuster Speakers Bureau at 1-866-248-3049 or visit our website at www.simonspeakers.com.

Also available in a Simon & Schuster Books for Young Readers hardcover edition

Cover design by Krista Vossen

Interior design by Hilary Zarycky

The text for this book was set in Adobe Garamond Pro.

Manufactured in the United States of America

0218 OFF

First Simon & Schuster Books for Young Readers paperback edition March 2018

2 4 6 8 10 9 7 5 3 1

The Library of Congress has cataloged the hardcover edition as follows:

Names: Gray, Kristin L., author

Title: Vilonia Beebe takes charge / Kristin L. Gray.

Description: First edition. | New York : Simon & Schuster Books for Young Readers, [2017] | "A Paula Wiseman Book." | Summary: "Vilonia must prove she is responsible enough to get a dog in order to help her mom get over her grief"—Provided by publisher.

Identifiers: LCCN 2016010814| ISBN 9781481458429 (hc)

| ISBN 9781481458443 (eBook)

Subjects: CYAC: Responsibility—Fiction. | Mothers and daughters–Fiction. | Grief—Fiction.

| BISAC: JUVENILE FICTION / Animals / Dogs. | JUVENILE FICTION / Family / Parents. |

JUVENILE FICTION / Social Issues / Depression & Mental Illness.

Classification: LCC PZ7.1.G734 Vi 2017 | DDC [Fic]—dc23

LC record available at https://lccn.loc.gov/2016020651

ISBN 9781481458436 (pbk)

For my family,
I love you more than cake.

And in memory of Eloise Ann Owen (2006–2016),
Vilonia would have picked you for her team every time.

"Do you think everybody misses somebody? Like I miss my mama?"

"Mmmm-hmmm," said Gloria. She closed her eyes. "I believe, sometimes, that the whole world has an aching heart."

—Kate DiCamillo, *Because of Winn-Dixie*

Chapter One

The day I was born I was four times smaller than the trophy largemouth bass hanging in my daddy's shop.

My entire hand fit on Dr. Lafferty's thumbnail. Nobody, Mama included, had planned on me arriving three months early.

But I did. At two pounds, two ounces, I was the size of a head of cauliflower (I hate cauliflower) and didn't make a peep. Boy, have times changed.

I pulled the cap off my gel pen, crossed out another line in my journal, and smudged purple ink all across the page. *Poodles.* More permanent ink stains, or as I call it, "the curse of being a lefty." But being left-handed could be pretty great. Lefties make better videogamers and multitaskers, adjust faster to seeing underwater, and have an advantage in many sports.

Maybe that's why lots of interesting people were lefties. Babe Ruth. Oprah Winfrey. Barack Obama. Me. So I wasn't A-list famous, but I was the only lefty on my hometown's ten-and-under softball team, the Howard County Crush. That had to count for something. I mean, I *had* played first base for three full seasons, and now Coach said I could try pitching. So what if star arm Mags Baloney moved to Texas to join some elite traveling team? I hadn't been this excited since our sponsor, Guy's Pies and Shakes, introduced the Crushin' Cookie Dough Blast in our honor. They promised everyone on the team free kiddie sizes, *all* season long.

So far my spring looked plumb awesome. Thank heavens. Because the last two months stunk worse than my brother, Leon, when he forgot to wear deodorant. He was twelve and impossible.

Speaking of which, writing this tribute to my nana proved impossible too. She'd been dead for forty-three days, and we still hadn't run her obituary. Mama had been in one sad funk ever since, and spent more time under the covers than out.

"Vilonia! Game's in twenty!" Daddy hollered from somewhere downstairs.

"Coming!" I yelled back, slamming my journal shut and pulling my jersey over my head. Nana's tribute would have to wait, again.

I tugged my visor onto my forehead and stopped to check my reflection in the bathroom mirror. *Howard County Crush* blazed across the front of my uniform in royal blue script, popping against the vibrant orange cloth. So did my last name, BEEBE (pronounced Bee-bee), and number, 10, that Daddy ironed on straight across the back. Hallelujah. Ten was a nice even number. I was almost ten. Almost double digits.

I smudged eye black across my cheeks and grabbed an orange ribbon for my hair. A fact about me: Normally, I wouldn't be caught dead (no offense to Nana) with a ribbon of any sort in my hair. Except for softball. This game blended girly and fierce.

Daddy called me his "force of nature." He says I talk faster, and louder, than a car salesman guzzling his third tall coffee. Which was why he always refused to take me fishing. Daddy was a fishing guide, and people who talk too much scare away the catch. You'd think being a force of nature would help.

But it hadn't helped me help Mama. It hadn't even helped me get a dog.

"Vilonia!"

Oops.

I hustled outside where Daddy, dressed in gray flannel and three days' worth of stubble, lugged a cooler down from the bed of his pickup.

"It's a perfect day to play ball!" I held my arms out to the sun, and a cool breeze brushed my face. It was the Thursday afternoon before spring break. Nana loved spring. "Nana would love today."

"She sure would, Tadpole. She loved to watch you play." Daddy reached into the cab of his truck and tossed my lucky glove my way. I snatched it midair and ran my fingers across its smooth leather.

"And what about Mama?" I asked, and stabbed the dirt with my toe. "Think she'll feel like coming?"

Daddy's eyes changed from sunny to cloudy with a chance of rain. "The forecast changes daily when it comes to Mama, Vi. But I can ask. You know she's your biggest fan."

"I know." I tried to hide my disappointment. I knew Daddy was doing his absolute best to take care of us, Mama included. But I've learned grief has no rules. She'll make herself at home, eat all your best snacks, sleep in your bed, and no matter what you do or say, sometimes nothing on earth can make her leave.

Daddy mussed my hair. "Your biggest fan next to me, that is. I'll be there by the third inning. Got to clean up first. I refuse to smell like bait while my best girl pitches her first game."

"Stink bait or not, I'll just be warming up." I threw him a fake pitch. "Fish for dinner?"

"Maybe. Now scoot." Daddy shooed me away with his cap and grinned. I smiled back. Daddy had the widest, most contagious grin in all of Mississippi. I had it on good authority. Mine.

"I'll be looking for ya." I snatched my bike—Leon's hand-me-down that I wrapped in paw-printed duct tape—from its usual spot in the yard and sped away.

The scent of honeysuckles hung thick in the air. I breathed

in their delicious smell and zipped past my best friend and next-door neighbor Ava Claire Nutter's house. Their American flag, long faded by the sun, waved a happy hello.

"Hey, Vilonia! Come over after dinner, okay?" AC, wearing her black leotard and sweats straight from dance, flitted to her mailbox. Ava Claire loved dance like lizards love sun.

"Okay!" I yelled, giving her a thumbs-up. Pedaling faster, I rounded the corner onto Hamilton and cruised downhill to the two-way stop.

My breath caught, and I skidded to a stop.

A big, fat chicken strode across the sunny intersection. Normally, I'd crack my why'd the chicken cross the road joke, but this wasn't any old rogue hen. This was Mrs. Willoughby's prize egg layer.

"Eleanor Roosevelt, you get back here right this instant!" Eleanor stopped, took one look at me, and then took off running. Hens could be so hardheaded. "You just wait!" I shouted. "You're going to be in one heap of troub—"

A white work van with a clanging ladder on its side barreled over the top of the hill, cutting off my words. *Shoot.* I turned to look at Eleanor. She'd stalled in the center of the road for an insect feast. Meanwhile, the van's driver bit into a sandwich. I'd landed a front row seat to a literal game of chicken.

"Run, Ellie, *run!*" I gripped my handlebars and squeezed my eyes shut, praying against a destruction of fender and feathers. Oblivious, the van roared through the intersection.

5

My heart pounded. I opened my eyes as the vehicle zoomed around the bend. Silence.

"Ellie?"

A few feathers floated back and forth, back and forth above the steamy pavement.

That hen was a goner.

"Poodles." I threw my bike to the ground. My eyes scanned the curb for any sign of the bird. Maybe she was still alive. It was a far-fetched hope, but Nana always said that hope was the thing with feathers. Looking both ways, I crossed the street. I walked up and down the sidewalk, trampling weeds with my cleats and calling out Eleanor's name. I had less than ten minutes until the first pitch, but it was my moral duty as eyewitness and decent human being to at least look for her. I couldn't leave a wounded critter behind.

"Eleanor?" I called.

But there was no sign of the rogue hen.

Maybe she flew to safety or maybe she flew straight to chicken heaven. Drat! Now Mama would be even sadder. She swore Eleanor's fresh eggs with their deep orange yolks were what made her sour cream pound cakes so velvety rich. I kicked the curb and walked back to my bike. And that's when I heard the cluck-clucking. I spun around on my heels and looked up. Way up.

That big chicken had perched in a tree.

"Eleanor, you silly bird. You about gave me a heart attack. Now get down here."

Another fact about me: I had never caught a chicken. I reckoned catching one's even harder when the hen's six feet up. According to the Willoughby boys, the trick was to grab them real stealth-like by the ankles. Chicken ankles. *Chankles.* I'd laughed.

I wasn't laughing now, waiting for Eleanor to come down. "Come *on*! Don't you care I have a game?" Eleanor wiggled her wattle and blinked. I shook the tree's trunk. But Eleanor flapped her wings in protest.

I looked around my feet and grabbed the first pebble I saw and chunked it close but not too close, hoping to spook her down. No such luck. Eleanor Roostevelt was one stubborn bird.

"Fine," I huffed. "I'll climb this tree faster than you can say *bawk bawk.*"

A few scrapes and scratches later, I had Eleanor under my arm. Her right leg stuck out at a weird angle, so I ended up grabbing her from behind as gently as I could. She clucked and flapped herself silly, but I held her wings down like the Willoughby boys had taught me.

"I've got you, Big E. It's going to be okay." I patted her back to calm her. I even wrapped my softball towel across her wings so she'd feel cozy and safe. As she nestled next to my glove inside my handlebar basket, I knew what I had to do.

I had to miss my game.

Chapter Two

I steered my bike several blocks to a brick-faced building with a weathered sign that read BEST F IENDS ANIMAL C INIC, DR. ROY KIEKLACK. An old oak with dangling bird feeders provided shade for much of the yard. Kickstand in place, I scooped up Eleanor, still bundled in the towel, and pushed open the glass door.

The COME IN sign clinked on its small chain as the door slipped shut. Dr. Kieklack's waiting room was bright and sterile like a hospital. And smelled like one too. I'd know because my memory from infancy was brilliant.

At the *whoosh* of the door, the receptionist, Miss Hazel Sogbottom, looked up over her bedazzled spectacles and popped a humongous wad of bubblegum. If anyone deserved a legal name change it was Miss Sogbottom.

"Good afternoon, Vilonia!" she said, taking a big sip of energy drink.

It's always awkward bumping into people for the first time

since Nana died. They don't know what to say: "How's your mama?" "Are y'all holding up?" Or the classic, "Your nana's in a better place." Even worse, some people flat go out of their way to avoid me or give me stuff out of pity. Like the time AC and I rode our bikes to the vegetable stand, and the farmer who usually waited on Mama got so flustered, he gave us two huge bags of asparagus for free. Our pee stunk for a solid week. All that to say it was a relief when someone acted normal. But even normal was a stretch for Miss Sogbottom.

"Hi." I shuffled up to the desk. Behind the counter, a red dachshund yipped and growled in his crate. In a flash, Miss Sogbottom turned and snapped her fingers. "Hush, T-Bone."

Spinning back to me, she smiled. Her spray-tanned cheeks sparkled with a hint of body glitter. "Someone's a little cranky after his ear drops."

"Oh." My eyes widened.

"He'll survive." She jammed a pencil into her hair-as-big-as-Texas and peered over the counter. "What have you got for us today? Another baby squirrel? A malnourished kitty?" So, I had a reputation for taking in destitute creatures. It all started when I adopted a nest of baby skunks last spring. I'd found the babies under our front porch after their mama got run over by a car. Mama wouldn't let me bring the kits (that's what you call baby skunks) indoors even though I showed her solid research saying most don't spray until they're three months old. So on the porch they stayed in a big cardboard box destined to prove

Mama right. And science wrong. These kits were advanced.

Still, it wasn't my fault the preacher's wife chose this week to bring over a Dutch apple pie. She spooked those skunks silly when she stomped mud off her boots right next to their box. Maybe she should have worn cleaner boots. Or looked before she stomped. No one touched the pie, and poor Mrs. Pounders smelled like skunk for three Sundays straight. Not to brag, but I did become the talk of the church potluck.

"It's nothing like that, Miss Sogbottom. It's the Willoughbys' hen, Eleanor Roostevelt." I held up Eleanor, still cloaked in my towel. "She's victim to a hit-and-run."

Miss Sogbottom clicked her tongue. "Got spooked and flew the coop again, I bet. You know those Willoughby boys and their firecrackers. I'll call Mrs. Willoughby to let her know we've got her."

It's true. The Willoughbys owned Tom Sawyer's Catfish Hole, a family-style restaurant that served up the best cat-fish filets your mouth ever did meet, *and* they ran the only fireworks stand for twenty-five miles. Believe me, those boys tested every black cat, smoke bomb, and parachute the day inventory rolled in.

"Thanks." I passed Eleanor over the counter, towel and all. She clucked loudly as if to say *Watch it, buster.* "Yeah." I frowned. "Her right leg doesn't look so good."

"Dr. Kieklack will take a look, don't you worry. Eleanor's what we call a frequent flyer; she's used to us. See?"

Sure as snail snot, Eleanor calmed down in the receptionist's arms. "You did right by bringing her in, Vilonia. She could have been snatched by a predator, you know. Here's your towel."

"Oh, right. Well, tell Dr. Kieklack hello. I've got a game to catch." I started to leave, but a poster on the wall jumped out at me. With my hand still on the doorknob, I read:

FEELING BLUE?
The most powerful antidepressant has
4 paws and a tail.
Pets promote well-being. Adopt yours today.
Contact the Howard County
Animal Shelter for details. 555-PETS

Then a photo of a yawning gray kitten cuddled up to a Labrador retriever with a softball in his mouth closed the deal: We Beebes needed a dog like Mama needed to feel better.

"You know," Miss Sogbottom said, "we partner with the shelter and have animals available for adoption here, too. Take T-bone, for example." T-bone growled.

"Ha, I wish." My cheeks grew hot, and I read the poster again. "Do you think pets *really* help with depression?"

"Absolutely," Miss Sogbottom said, cradling Eleanor like a football. "Pets provide comfort and companionship. They can make people laugh. They don't care if you forget to turn in your homework or don't feel like brushing your hair. They love you regardless." The receptionist pointed to a framed photo of a rabbit sitting on her desk. "My mini lop Oreo has seen me through hard times and heartbreaks." She looked at me quizzically. "Are you sure you're okay, Vilonia?" *Oh boy.* She didn't know Mama had come down with the Infinite Sadness, and I had no time to explain. No time to explain I needed a dog now more than ever.

"I'm just fine, Miss Sogbottom. Thanks and good-bye. Bye, Eleanor!" I blurted instead.

"Buh-bye." Miss Sogbottom waved over her shoulder as she whisked Ellie to the back. "And go, team!"

Heart racing, I rode like the wind on the best kite-flying day. If Eleanor Roostevelt hadn't crossed the road in front of me, I'd never have read that poster. If I hadn't read that poster, I wouldn't know how badly we needed a dog. No one plans on rescuing a chicken and discussing heartbreak right before her first ballgame of the season. But I hadn't planned on arriving at the ballpark and debating this word either:

Forfeit.

Daddy arrived at the ballpark in time to drive my bike and sorry self home. "Vilonia, please pay attention," he said as we walked into the kitchen. "You know the rules. Six players on the field at game time. They were counting on you."

"I know, Daddy, but Phoebe and Summer weren't there

either! And Eleanor Roostevelt needed prompt medical attention. What's more important?" My face felt splotched.

Daddy poured us each a glass of cold milk and ignored the stack of dirty dishes filling Mama's stainless sink. She loved that sink—back when she enjoyed cooking. "Phoebe and Summer had their family vacations approved weeks ago. Just no more found creatures, okay? We're a family. We're not running some animal rescue operation."

"But, Daddy."

"Don't 'but, Daddy' me. Vilonia, last week you hid a peacock. In our *basement*. He ruined your nana's velvet couch!"

"How would I know Steve had escaped from a petting zoo?"

Daddy ran his fingers across his uneven beard and sighed. "You're a smart girl, Vilonia. Use your noodle."

My noodle. My noggin. My brain. The one they were so worried about when I was born ten weeks too early. I did use it, and Daddy had no idea how much. There was this side job I sort of fell into. It was 100 percent hush-hush. Number one, I could get Mama in trouble because it was really *her* job. She hasn't been able to write a single thing since Nana died. (I knew because I was watching videos of those fainting goats when a work e-mail came through stating Mama would be replaced if she didn't write *something*.) And two, no one, not Mama or Daddy or Mama's boss, knew I was doing it. I was writing the county obits.

Obits, or obituaries, are paragraph summaries of dead

people. They appear online or in the paper and make nice people out to be super nice and not-so-nice people out to be better than they actually were. For the most part.

When you spend your free time writing about the newly dead, it's best to keep a sense of humor. This biz can and will suck the life right out of you. At least that's what Mama says, and look where it got her.

Daddy whistled and waved a hand in front of my face. "And Leon found this by the tire swing."

Great Danes and greyhounds! Peon Leon had found my long-lost library book. I'd only checked it out a gazillion times before it'd disappeared. Shoot, *Because of Winn-Dixie* was the whole reason I started the Great Pet Campaign in the first place. I'd have traded my lucky softball socks to have a dog half as good as him. Of course, I'd searched Pet Campaign Headquarters (aka my room) and emptied my desk at school and never came across the book. Until now.

The only problem was *Because of Winn-Dixie*'s hardcover, featuring India Opal and her smiling mutt, now looked warped beyond repair. Its pages showed that trademark wave of having been dropped in a puddle of water, the bathtub (don't ask), or in this case, left out in the rain. I knew because I'd last seen it the day of the rainout. The day I took my first obit. The day Scooter Malone of Howard County, beloved father, grandfather, and friend, died of congestive heart failure while playing a game of checkers. He was seventy-nine.

Dad handed over the book and sighed. "You'll need to pay Mr. Reyes for it, using your allowance."

I picked at the ruined corner. "You mean my *pet* fund." Maybe Mr. Reyes, my school librarian, wouldn't drain my whole twenty-eight dollars and three cents.

"Vilonia, we've discussed this before. We absolutely cannot get a dog—or any pet for that matter. Your mama can't handle anything else right now . . . You've got to start taking care of your things and showing your mama and me more—"

"I know, responsibility." I shot Leon a dirty look. He'd been mouthing along with Daddy's speech. Yeah, we were all tired of hearing it, but no one more than me. Doggone it, I *was* responsible. I brushed my teeth with minty fluoride cavity-fighting toothpaste every stinking night, thank you very much. And I hadn't lost my new rain jacket yet. I'd had it three whole weeks. That had to be a world record. It was navy with green frogs and perfect for fishing in the rain. Did I mention I hadn't even lost it?

This week alone, I'd taken out the trash, cleared the table without being asked, and *ta-da!* accepted a new role at school as the Friday Library Helper.

But this wasn't the time to mention that. So instead, I trudged upstairs to HQ, where my "You can always trust a dog that likes peanut butter" *Winn-Dixie* poster clung to the door.

More dog posters covered the walls inside. And sticky notes. A sticky note for every reason I should have a dog. I had over thirty squares on the wall at the moment. Dogs make good friends. Dogs keep you active. Dogs can sense danger. I whipped out a fat orange marker and jotted down one more: Dogs soothe aching hearts.

Sitting on my bed, I sifted through notes from family members regarding the week's deceased. The really weird part was when they sent in photos of left-behind pets. They were almost always cats.

Twirling the marker in one hand, I got to work highlighting important information. One woman had visited a hundred national parks before her ninety-ninth birthday. Another had played the organ at her church for over thirty years and occasionally enjoyed skydiving. Neither of those are what killed her. Pneumonia did.

I got the obits written and e-mailed them, from Mama's account, to the editor of the Howard County Press. Once printed, I'd paste them inside my obituary scrapbook, the two-inch binder I sneakily labeled ANTHROPOLOGY.

When I couldn't think anymore, I shut the book in favor of skimming India Opal's story, even though I knew it by heart. I mean she (spoiler alert!) did convince the preacher to let her keep Winn-Dixie. I just needed to find the right dog to convince *my* dad.

But getting Daddy to agree to a dog would take a miracle similar to the birth of sweet baby Jesus. A sick feeling swam in my gut. I'd have to try flattery, then possibly hypnosis. At the very least, I needed some heavy-duty research. More than I did with the skunks.

"Hey, Vi! We've got a bit of a situation!" Ugh, *Leon*.

"Good grief." I capped the orange marker ever so *responsibly* so it wouldn't ruin my comforter and zipped downstairs with my book. "I told you I was busy. This had better be—*yum*."

The smell of cookies fresh from the oven stopped me in my tracks. Mama's big red mixing bowl was drying upside down on the counter. The pile of dishes had disappeared from the sink. My heart skipped a beat.

"Mama?"

"Wrong." Leon brushed by me with a metal box, filled to the brim with mouth-watering, delicious oatmeal chocolate-chip cookies as big as my face. I knew right off Daddy had baked them using Mama's recipe. Daddy added chocolate chips to every recipe whether it called for them or not.

Plus it'd been weeks since Mama had used an oven. Weeks since we'd sampled her legendary cookies and cakes. Sure, Mama's love for baking had spoiled us, but store-bought cookies didn't taste as good as her homemade ones. And have mercy if Leon ever tried to make them, the Fire Department would arrive in full force.

"Not so fast. Where's mine?" I asked.

Leon hooked his thumb toward the kitchen counter.

Three cookies cooled on the wire rack. "Oh, you shouldn't have."

"What?" Leon balked. "Dad took a few, and I'm keeping the rest safe by taking them to the track meeting. You should thank me." *Safe? Really?*

"Ha. Everyone knows you just want to impress your new coach."

"He's not my coach!" Leon held the tin of cookies out of my reach. "Yet." It was true. After last year's blow of not making the team, Leon resolved to wake up at six a.m. three times a week to run. And I don't mean to the donut shop.

I sprung for the cookies again. "Well, I am *this* close to telling Ransom Willoughby and the rest of the track team that you're a ginormous cookie thief who still sleeps with a stuffed frog." I put my hands on my hips and stuck out my chin. "Going to a track meeting is hardly 'a situation,' anyway. Besides, you don't even like oatmeal."

"I don't." My brother smirked. "But she does." Leon motioned to the kitchen window. A burgundy sedan with a busted-out headlight cut its engine in our drive. "The *situation* is she's been sitting out front for ten minutes."

"Ten minutes. Are you sure?"

Leon tapped his stopwatch. My palms began to sweat.

"What could she want?" *She* was Miss Bettina, newspaper editor and Mama's boss. I disliked her more than cauliflower.

Leon shrugged and lowered the tin for me to make my choice. "What she always wants. A story."

Or an *obit*.

I snatched the cookie with the most chocolate chips. It was still fall-apart hot. "You can't leave me here with her! She's nuts."

Leon checked his stopwatch. "Oh, yes I can." He snapped the lid on the cookies, pocketed an apple for himself, and jogged to the back door. "Watch me."

"Wait!" I stuck my head outside. "Where's Mama?"

"Sleeping."

"And Daddy?"

"In his shop."

"Poodles." I licked gooey chocolate from my fingertips and secured the back door. The last bite of cookie dissolved in my mouth as the all-too familiar voice drifted inside.

"Vilonia, honey, I know you're in there."

Chapter Three

I peeked through the side curtains framing our front door and snapped them shut. Yep. Only one person in all of Howard County wore floral prints the size of dinner plates.

"Vilonia?" Miss Bettina said again.

Maybe she'd put two and two together, see Daddy's boat was gone, and make like a tree and leave.

Knock. Knock.

Nope.

"Vilonia, this is important business. Right up there with the sheriff's wedding. Is your mama home?"

I groaned. Everything was important to Miss Bettina, especially when it was none of her business. I don't know why I opened that door. She buzzed in faster than a fly to jellied toast.

"Where's that mama of yours? Mrs. Tooley's kicked the can." Miss Bettina clapped her fingers together with glee. Only she would be thrilled when a member of our town passed on. That meant news to spew. She bowled by me in screaming hibiscus print, and honest to goodness, I tried to protest.

"Mama's resting," I said, following her into the kitchen. "She doesn't need to be bothered."

"Nonsense, Vilonia. This is Mrs. Tooley we're talking about. It'll be the biggest obit of the year!" She leaned close (a pet peeve of mine) and cackled. Her breath smelled of onions, garlic, and hush puppies. "Mmm." Miss Bettina closed her eyes and drew a deep breath. "I smell . . ."

I stole that second to position myself strategically between Mama's boss and the cooling rack.

"Cinnamon!" Her eyes flew open. She reached her arm around me and helped herself to a cookie. My cookie.

Now, Mama pretty much liked everyone in Howard County, Mississippi, and even though her job was to consult next of kin when writing our dearly departed's obituaries, I knew for a fact she already had a draft put back for her boss Bettina B. Wiggins. It wasn't scathing. But it wasn't overly kind.

Just like Miss Bettina.

"Do you think there'll be one of those fancy estate sales?" Her cheeks wobbled with excitement. "I'd love to get my hands on her iron skillets. Why, they're positively ancient." Leave it to Hush Puppy Breath to think of estate sales and skillets at a time like this. She popped my cookie into her cavernous mouth. "And did you hear about her pregnant dog, Harper?" she asked, spraying cookie bits in my general direction.

I shook my head, not sure I wanted to know.

"So grieved by her owner's death, the poor pup's gone into preterm labor. Have you ever heard of such a thing? In dogs, I mean?" I opened my mouth to answer I had not heard of such, but Miss Bettina kept on and helped herself to a second cookie. Now, I'm not the best at math, but I knew how many cookies that left.

"What about the puppies?" I asked, helping myself to the last cookie while the getting was good.

"I'm glad you asked." She tapped her fat finger against my chest, driving home each syllable. I stepped backward into my personal space. "Wilfred, her gardener, found the sweet thing whimpering under the front porch. Martha had the loveliest front porch, especially this time of year, when the lilacs bloom." She paused a moment to wipe at an invisible tear or maybe a cookie crumb. "Anyhow, Wilfred—that sweet, gentle soul—drove her immediately to the veterinarian, Dr. Kieklack. Have you ever met Dr. Kieklack? He guessed she had six pups inside. Of course, we're all just praying the young'uns survive. Have you any milk?" she asked, throwing open our refrigerator door like she lived here instead of us.

"Oh! I don't think we . . ."

Miss Bettina stared in silence at the contents of our fridge. The top shelf held a half stick of butter and, thanks to

Eleanor, six hard-boiled eggs. Two zucchini squash rattled in the vegetable crisper next to a wrinkled tomato, while a bag of golden delicious apples tried valiantly to fill the other drawer. An expired package of deli meat shared the middle shelf with last night's pizza leftovers and Daddy's catch of the day: catfish neatly filleted and marinating in a plastic bag. And in the door, a jar of Nana's blackberry jam made its home next to pickles, spicy brown mustard, and packets of takeout soy sauce. The spot for milk contained a near-empty carton of juice.

"We used up all of the milk this morning." I crossed my fingers behind my back.

Miss Bettina pinched her eyebrows together and frowned. "Something funny is going on, Vilonia." She shut the door and glanced around the kitchen. "Lookie here, your calendar is still on March."

"Well," I said, crossing the room to block the pantry—even though it was plenty stocked, because Mama bought baked goods in bulk. "Nana died, and we haven't thought to update the calendar."

Miss B's face softened like ice cream left in the sun. Pointing to my ruined library book, open on the table, she read its title. Of course she did. She read everything whether it belonged to her or not. "You know, Vilonia, if those puppies survive, they'll need homes."

What? My heart flopped like a fish in the bottom of Daddy's boat. "You mean adoptive homes? Like a pet, for keeps?"

"Are you interested?"

Does a bullfrog croak?

"Miss Bettina. As founder and chief financial officer of the Great Pet Campaign, I can assure you that's an affirmative. But as Terry and Janet Beebe's daughter, it's . . . complicated." I let out a sad sigh. After Daddy's lecture, I didn't dare bring up adopting a real live puppy. But the possibility of finding a puppy that's a preemie, like me? That made me giddy dizzy. "It's just, Opal and I have this thing in common." I nodded to the book's cover. "We have to convince our dads first." I swiped away stray cookie crumbs with the back side of my hand.

"I respect that. Puppies aren't for everyone." Miss Bettina's face turned serious as stone. "Especially preemies. They're fragile. They demand the best care, the most attention, and you must steel yourself, Vilonia, for the harsh reality he or she may not survive. If they come out alive to start with."

"Yes, ma'am." I swallowed and rubbed my thumb across the line of silver dots and dashes traveling the inside of my wrist. My story wounds. Leftover IV scars from my own stay in the hospital's special nursery for super-sick newborns. They called it the NICU, or Neonatal Intensive Care Unit.

"Well. If your daddy changes his mind, swing by Dr. Kieklack's and pick up an adoption sheet. No commitment, just a list of questions so they can get to know you. Now, if you could fetch your mama . . ." Miss Bettina wandered into the living room, plucked a stray sock off the back of the sofa, and inspected it. There was no doubt in my mind she would have sat right down had Laundry Mountain not occupied the space first. I steered the subject back to the puppies.

"Why would Dr. Kieklack need to know more about me?"

"To make sure the dog is going to a good home. Also, competition. It's possible someone else may want the same dog as you."

"Oh." Worry flapped like blackbirds inside my chest.

"Never fear." Miss Bettina smiled for a brief instant. "The dog chooses its owner, you know."

"No, I didn't know."

"All we can do is wait and wish Harper and her puppies the best. This part, it isn't left to us." That might be the wisest thing Miss Bettina's ever said—even wiser than, "A nose for news just knows."

I sat silent (unheard of, I know) and turned all this *news*—Mrs. Tooley, Wilfred, and the puppies-yet-to-be-born—over in my head. Meanwhile, Miss Bettina glanced at our wrinkled laundry, our wilting plant, and our coffee table with "Leon was here" written in its dust. As good as Daddy's homemade cookies were, her nose had to sense something was o-f-f.

Miss Bettina cleared her throat.

"Right!" I tiptoed down the hall to Mama's room. The door was shut. My hand found the knob, and the door clicked open. I peered through the crack.

"Mama?" I whispered. "You awake?" I crept across the

hardwood into the dark. Mama kept her curtains pulled tight, and my eyes needed a moment to adjust to the lack of light.

Mama, her back to me, was sound asleep. She wore her new uniform—the paisley pink pajamas we'd given her on Valentine's Day. Her nightstand held crinkled tissues, a framed wedding photo of her and Daddy, a glass of water, some pills, empty Little Debbie wrappers (Mama's favorite treat not baked from scratch), and one book, open and facedown. I squinted at the title. *A Grief Observed.* If anyone was observing Grief, it was me, now. Mama looked peaceful. Not sad. Not happy. But peaceful. I couldn't wake her. I wouldn't.

I slipped out and shut the door.

Miss Bettina bolted upright when I reappeared. She'd been crouched in front of our bookcase, reading all the spines. Snooping, was more like it.

"Miss Bettina." I smiled too big and waited for her to put the framed photograph she clutched back on the shelf. "Mama's not feeling well, but she says to e-mail her Mrs. Tooley's information, and she'll have a draft for you ASAP." I clasped my hands together and stuck my smile like Ava Claire sticks her dance routine.

"So, I can't *see* her?" Miss Bettina's huge eyes narrowed.

"Afraid not." My palms grew sweaty. I had to get Hush Puppy Breath and her nose for news out of here. "I hate to be rude, but I've got math homework up to my earlobes. Mrs. Crewel *loves* fractions." I yanked on my earlobes to drive the

26

point home. "The paper's probably missing you anyways."

"Oh my stars, yes. They can't function without me." Miss Bettina bustled to the front door, which I conveniently held open. "Next time, when your mama's feeling better, let's visit over a slice of her heavenly pound cake. Not that the cookies weren't scrumptious; they're just missing something."

Not some*thing*. Some*one*.

I smiled, ignoring her use of "next time."

"And I'll e-mail Mrs. Tooley's particulars, God rest her soul."

"Amen," I muttered as her burgundy sedan with the broken headlight screeched out of sight.

I itched to run next door and blab to Ava Claire about Miss Bettina's bizarre visit, but I couldn't. Leon would be home soon and hungry as five-and-a-half men. Daddy, too, if he didn't work until dark. . . . I dug through the freezer and found three mini chicken potpies, plus one turkey. It wasn't catfish and hush puppies, but it'd do.

Chapter Four

Friday morning, I tossed my money, the ruined library book, and another book I'd borrowed but thankfully left indoors, all into my backpack and headed downstairs.

Daddy met me at the bottom with my raincoat.

"Better wear this, Tadpole." He was weather obsessed. It came with being a fisherman.

"Daddy." I sighed and looked out the window to the bus stop. "No one else has one."

"Yet. Trust me."

I tugged the jacket on and gave him a quick kiss as I flew out the door. I made it to the end of the walk before the rain came. Pulling up the hood, I smirked. *Daddy, one point.* I snapped the buttons down the front and hoped the bus would still run on time. I loved Fridays, and Mr. Reyes expected me.

Leon sped by me to wait with the guys from the sixth-grade

track team. If only they knew how silly they looked, huddled together like ducks in matching pants. I zipped by unnoticed, or so I thought, until one of them quacked, "Hey, Vilonia." I stopped. Rory Willoughby, one of the Willoughby twins, with hair so wavy even the ocean was jealous, ran toward me. I bit my lip. Maybe he was going to ask me to prom. It was only five years away.

"Hey," I said, not noticing one bit that his cute freckles had migrated across the bridge of his nose and his eyes were now greener than a four-leaf clover.

He grinned. A row of metal flashed across his teeth, and my legs became spaghetti. "Thanks for rescuing Eleanor."

"Thanks for being so perfect."

"What?" He tilted his head.

"Perky!" I died faster than an armadillo crossing the highway. "Thanks for being so perky. Most people aren't morning material."

"Yeah. Well, thanks again." He smiled. I turned away and squinted through the raindrops, happy to see the bus's headlights peeping through the fog.

"Gotta run," I said.

"I'd sit toward the front of the bus if I were you," he said, and took off.

"Hey, Vilonia!" Ava Claire waved and shuffled up the walk next to me in full rain gear. Her dark cheeks flushed pink from the brisk morning air. "What was that about?"

29

"I'm not exactly sure." I shrugged and pointed to the rosy tulle poking out beneath her daisy raincoat. "Really, AC? It's raining, in case you missed it."

"In case *you* missed it, it's Career Day in Mr. Manning's class. Anyway, weather doesn't stop me. I've got rain boots."

And she did. She probably had a matching umbrella in her backpack too.

Ava Claire was all ruffles and tutus and sparkly dance shoes—everything I wasn't. I'd played softball since I could swing a bat, but Ava Claire wasn't interested the minute she laid her brown eyes on those "ugly spiked shoes." She'd rather twirl onstage in scratchy sequins under one-thousand-watt lights. Yeah, we went together like toothpaste and orange juice, but if anyone tried picking on either one of us, we stuck together like gum to a shoe.

"Hey," she said again, plopping down in the seat beside mine. "You didn't come over last night."

"I know. Sorry." I pressed my back against the window and stretched my legs out across the seat. "We forfeited our game—long story—and then Miss Bettina dropped by." I sighed. AC would have me over every day of the week if she could.

"Bummer. It's okay." Her mouth twisted into a frown, and she reached for the silver locket around her neck. "He didn't call."

Poodles! I can't believe I forgot to ask.

"And"—she paused, turning her locket over—"it's been five weeks since he wrote."

It was my turn to frown. No wonder she watched for the mail every day. I looked at the locket General Nutter had given his daughter before he was deployed to Afghanistan nine months ago. "Well. I'm sure he's okay. Just busy, you know. Bringing peace to the world."

"Maybe you're right." She let go of the necklace. Her face brightened. "Neely's hopeful he'll be home soon. Maybe in time for the Catfish Festival next weekend." So, AC called her mother by her first name. She insisted "Neely" sounded more professional and helped her drum up clients for her nail salon.

"The Festival! That'd be great," I said. "Maybe he'll catch your dance for the pageant! And I know how much the general loves fish. He's always one of the first in line at the Willoughbys' food truck."

"Yeah," she gushed. "I still can't believe I was asked to dance. They had a last-minute cancellation and invited *me* on Miss Connelly's recommendation." She let out a dreamy sigh. "It's just a transition number while the contestants change costumes, but it's still *onstage* at Miss Catfish!" My best friend squealed so high only dogs could hear.

"And I'll be in the front row, cheering you on. I can paint my face and bring one of those giant foam fingers that say 'number one fan.'"

"Vilonia, this isn't baseball. And the general would get

dibs on the foam sign anyway." She frowned. "Not that I'm getting my hopes up that the general will be there, but it's hard not to, you know?"

Boy, did I. An image of Mama humming in the kitchen with her hair pulled back, icing a gigantic three-layer cake, with a dab of frosting on her cheek, and our dog-to-be sound asleep at her feet flashed through my mind. I reached out and squeezed AC's hand. "I know."

She squeezed back. "So, Miss Bettina came to your house?"

"Yeah. She wanted to talk about Mrs. Tooley." I slashed my finger across my throat.

"Oh." AC's eyes grew wide. She knew Mama's job was to write the obituaries. She didn't know Mama had help. As interesting as obituaries were, I did not want to write them forever. I leaned my head against the glass and pulled my bag to my chest. I was just giving Mama a hand until she felt better, which she would, with a little help from a dog.

The bus jolted and turned onto Madison Street, right past the park.

"Ugh. What's that smell?" AC wrinkled her nose. "Rotten eggs?"

"I don't smell any—Skunk!" I pulled my jacket up over my nose and gagged. "They smell worse than Leon's PE uniform. Quick! Open your window." My eyes began to water. Kids on either side of us groaned and gagged. AC grabbed her nose. The little boy in front of me asked for help with his window. Bus windows, like molasses, were sticky business.

Everywhere I looked, kids scrambled over one another to get a breath of fresh air. Someone mentioned the words "stink bomb." And I remembered Rory's words, *I'd sit toward the front of the bus if I were you.*

Those Willoughbys. Ransom and Rory had the three characteristics necessary for pulling off and getting away with pranks: mischief, charm, and dashing good looks. Not to mention their family's fireworks stand. Of course those boys had stink bombs. I looked to the back of the bus, hoping to catch Rory's eye, but Mr. Danny, our bus driver who's older than dirt but somehow still has his driver's license, came over the loudspeaker.

"I need everyone to listen up and sit down. I've survived two hurricanes, a wife, and a war. I'm getting y'all to school safe and sound. Ya' hear?"

One voice rose above the crowd.

"Ick! Move outta my way! A girl's got to breathe."

AC, still pinching her nose, looked at me and rolled her eyes.

DeeAnne Druxbury, in her designer raincoat and boots, pushed past me to the front of the bus like she was an angry hornet. "Ransom and Rory Willoughby, I ought to have you both expelled."

Ransom, the firstborn by a whole four minutes and often the instigator, piped up from the back of the bus, "But we didn't step on it, DeeAnne. You did."

The bus roared with laughter.

Mr. Danny grabbed his microphone. "Miss Druxbury, I drove your daddy's bus before he ever thought of becoming mayor, and if you don't sit yourself down, I'll drive you straight to his office."

Lo and behold, she plopped herself down by Dawson O'Dell, an aspiring actor who at the moment looked three shades of green—he's just that good—and said, "Open your window, Dawson! If you puke on me, you *will* buy me a new raincoat."

"If I puke on you, you probably deserve it. And your coat's waterproof."

Mercifully, the bus lurched to a stop one block from school. The doors whooshed open. Mr. Danny didn't have to tell us twice. We jammed through the doors like the bus had caught cooties. Walking away, I heard the old driver click his tongue and mutter, "Kids these days. Now, let me see what's causing this mess."

Mr. Reyes was already checking in books at the circulation desk when I knocked on the door. He looked up, smiled his lopsided grin, and waved me in.

The competition to become Library Helper had been fierce, but in the end, I was the lucky fourth grader whose name he drew out of his glittering World's Best Librarian mug. So I entered twenty-one times, but who's counting?

Mr. Reyes picked *me* to be his student volunteer every single Friday morning before the first bell.

On a normal day, I'd float across that floor. I loved our library. I loved feeding Maximus Tropicana, Mr. Reyes's goldfish, a little copper ray of sun swimming laps atop the circulation desk. I loved processing returned books. I loved reading the titles, thumbing through the pages as I placed them back on the shelves. Most of all, I loved that book smell.

But today, I hesitated.

"If it isn't Miss Beebe, reader extraordinaire," Mr. Reyes exclaimed, moving a stack of graphic novels to the cart for shelving. He'd worn his usual Friday uniform—red Converse, jeans, and a faded Captain America tee. It was easy as pie to love Mr. Reyes. He was the coolest, which was why it was even harder to disappoint him. "So tell me, Vilonia. Do you have big spring break plans?"

"I wish. I may be getting a dog, though. Only he hasn't been born yet." I dropped my backpack to the floor and started to shed my raincoat. My fingers fumbled nervously over the snaps.

"A new dog's plenty exciting," Mr. Reyes offered.

"Yeah. It's not definite, but I thought maybe I should do some research first."

"Great idea. I can help you look." He walked around the desk.

"Oh! No, that's okay." I waved him off. "I got it, Mr. Reyes, but I do need to show you something." I placed *Winn-Dixie* on the desk and winced. "Leon found it. I'm really sorry."

"I see." Mr. Reyes inspected the book's cover and interior while whistling the Spider-Man theme. Across the hall, a mob of students exited the lunchroom. *Time for class.*

"Decided to go for a swim, did we?" He winked.

"Not exactly." My face burned. "I left it outside by accident. I read a lot on the tire swing." I wanted nothing more than to hide behind the E-Z reader shelf. *Way to go, Vi.* Get selected Library Helper, and the very next book you return's DOA, dead on arrival. I'd already begun writing the obit in my head:

> *Because of Winn-Dixie*, written by Kate DiCamillo, was first published in 2000 and one hundred and ninety-two pages long. Dog-eared and underlined, this beloved hardcover was checked out over one hundred and forty-eight times before it met its demise sometime after Friday, March 4, under a tire swing on Walleye Street. Memorial donations may be sent to Howard County Elementary School, c/o Mr. Reyes.

More kids crowded the hall outside, laughing and pushing their way to class. A few jostled their way inside the library. One kid in a striped beanie strode up to the counter and waited to speak.

"I brought money to pay for it," I said.

"Let's see how much it is, first." Mr. Reyes scratched his forehead and smiled. "You aren't the first or the last student to leave a book outside." He turned to the kid in the hat. "Good morning, Ian. What'd your folks say about keeping Max?"

Ian shook his head. "Sorry, Mr. Reyes. We're going to my grandma's."

"It's okay. Next time." Mr. Reyes smiled, and Ian left with his friends.

Winn-Dixie disappeared under the counter. Mr. Reyes disappeared into his tiny office.

I scanned the barcode of my other book and added it to the return cart. The clock above the circulation desk read 7:50.

I had a few moments alone to research, and then I needed to go to class. I went to the nearest computer and typed "dogs and sadness" into the search box. A few titles appeared.

Six Ways Pets Can Help Us Cope. Hope and Healing through Dog Companionship. The Healing Power of Pets . . . yada yada. I went to the shelf, pulled a title down, and flipped through the pages. *"Doctors know that simply watching fish in an aquarium can soothe an anxious person and lower her blood pressure." Huh.* Maybe that's why Dr. Stacy has an aquarium. I shuddered, thinking of my back-to-school shots, and quickly skipped ahead to the chapter on dogs. *"Mild to moderate depression can be treated by adopting a dog, as dogs are loyal, lifelong companions . . . Curious and charming, dogs provide daily structure and a reason to get out of bed. Dogs require responsibility. They need to eat, play, and go for walks . . ."*

There it was again. Responsibility. But I knew if given a chance, a dog could soothe Mama's soul like a slice of warm butterscotch pie: the perfect swirl of salty and sweet in one delicious bite. Still, it felt good to see it in print. But how would I get Daddy to agree?

The warning bell sounded. I reshelved the book and waltzed past the circulation desk and Max, still swimming laps, to tell Mr. Reyes I was done. Then it hit me: Max could be my ticket to responsibility. If I could keep a fish happy and fed for a week, then surely Daddy would see the light and agree to get a dog. We'd all be a lot better off. And by "we" I meant Mama.

Mr. Reyes stood hunched over his keyboard, deep in thought. His desk was a chaotic mess of stacked books, papers, and discarded coffee cups. On the wall behind him a huge Harry Potter poster exclaimed DON'T BE A MUGGLE. READ GOOD BOOKS.

"Mr. Reyes?" My voice cracked. "I overheard part of your conversation with Ian. Do you, uh, need someone to watch Max over spring break?"

"Ah, Vilonia! Sorry, I got distracted. Last day before spring break and all." He smiled and folded his arms across his chest. "I *do* need a sitter for Max for spring break. Are you interested?"

It seemed like a harmless question. I mean, how hard could babysitting a fish be?

"I thought it might be good practice in case I get a dog."

Mr. Reyes glanced past me at a student who'd wandered in. "Be right there, Keisha." Then, turning back to me, he smiled. "I think you are absolutely right. Why don't you call home during lunch to make sure it's okay with your parents." Mr. Reyes jotted a quick note to my teacher and tossed his pen back onto his desk.

I skimmed the message right as the bell rang: *Please send Vilonia to the library the last ten minutes of class. —TR*

"Thank you, Mr. Reyes. Don't forget to tell me what I owe for the book." I ran breathless out the door, amazed by my great luck, only to circle back. "Forgot my bag. See you later!"

Mr. Reyes waved. I might as well change my name to Dork.

Fifteen minutes before the last bell, Mrs. Crewel said I was free to go. I think she grew tired of me bouncing in my seat. I still couldn't believe Mama had picked up the phone and said yes when I'd called to ask about Max. I paid Mr. Reyes twelve one-dollar bills to replace the book. He gave me pointers on Max, how much food to feed him and when (one piece in the morning, another in the afternoon). This was cake.

The three p.m. bell rang, and one huge *Whoop!* echoed through the halls.

"Have a good break, you two."

"Oh, we will," I said, cradling Max in my arms. "I'll take great care of him, you'll see."

As usual, AC had saved me the seat across from her and

right behind the Willoughbys, whom I hoped had no more surprises. Luckily, Mr. Danny had left the windows down all day so the bus would air out.

AC's mouth fell open when she saw me.

"You're taking Max home?"

"Yep. I'm fish sitting for Mr. Reyes over break."

"Cool." She tapped on the glass with her polished fingernail. Max darted away.

"Yeah." I slid by the window so Max could see out.

"I wouldn't mention the fates of most fish at your house," AC added as the bus rumbled out of the school lot.

"He's a goldfish, AC, not a catfish. What could happen?"

We were the first stop.

"Look, Max," I said, smudging my finger against the glass. "There's your new home."

Chapter Five

"My room's a bit different from the library," I said, standing in my doorway after giving Max a house tour. "But I bet you'll like it. There are still tons of books. And dog posters and sticky notes galore." Max bobbed to the surface. "And over here are my softball trophies and my giant plush dog named Kitty. He smiles like Winn-Dixie. And out this window you can see my tree house. Maybe I'll take you to see it."

Max peered through the glass into my bedroom, soaking up his new view. The pale blue walls were the color of sky on a clear day. I didn't tell him Mama had helped me paint them, ceiling too, a week before the phone call. A week before the fog rolled in. I didn't mention that it was the last fun thing we'd done together.

I set Max down on my desk and moved a teetering stack of books blocking the window to the floor.

"There. You can see AC's house from here. Some fish

would pay good money to see Neely back her car down the drive. She's hit the mailbox four times this year."

Max looked at me, his eyes big and unsure.

"Hey, you need a housewarming present." I pointed to the group of seashells on my desk. "Eenie. Meenie. Miney. Moe. Let's spiff up your boring bowl."

I dropped a conch into the tank. *Plink!* Max darted to the side while the shell settled to the bottom. I'm no decorator, but the conch looked pretty cozy on Max's blue gravel, like something in a photograph. I knew right away Mr. Reyes would approve. And I was positive that given another day, Max would learn to love it too.

Later, after the dishes were scrubbed and showers were taken and Leon had started battling pre-algebra, Daddy and I moved our root beers to the family room to tackle Laundry Mountain. Which was really code for us watching the Weather Channel.

"Start wishing for good weather at the Catfish Festival next weekend. Remember last year?"

"How could I forget? We practically floated home."

"Well, 'the weather *is* a great bluffer.'"

I shook my head. Daddy loved to remind me of a favorite author E. B. White's idea about weather.

"Hey," Leon called from the dining room, "maybe you'll be tall enough to ride some *real* rides!"

"Hey, aren't you supposed to be doing homework?" I shot

back, and made a mental note to check my height before bed.

"Guys, I'm trying to listen." Daddy hushed us, then shook wrinkles out of an undershirt. "How can he say a twenty percent chance of precipitation tomorrow? Did he see the same clouds I did?"

I rolled up a pair of socks. "Did *you* see our new house guest?"

"What house guest?" Daddy whipped his head around, looking for a stray skunk.

"The one on the counter." I fished another sock from the laundry basket. "You know how you said I need to become more responsible?"

"Yesss. . . ." Daddy shot me a look. I dug through the clean clothes, focused on finding the sock's mate.

"Well. Mr. Reyes needed someone to keep the library goldfish over spring break."

Daddy turned toward me. "And?"

"And I thought maybe it'd be great practice for a real pet. Someday. In the future." I smiled my most convincing smile. "What's the forecast for that?"

Daddy pulled Leon's track pants from the heap and folded them in half. "The forecast says there's a ninety percent chance you buttered me up."

"So I can keep him?" I tossed the socks into the air and hugged his scruffy neck.

"Yes." He laughed. "Just this week."

"Good, because Mama already said yes. Don't you worry, Daddy. This week's gonna be great."

Before bed, I returned the laundry basket to the laundry room. Up and down the doorframe, pencil scratches recorded my and Leon's heights and ages over the years. Immediately, my heart ached *Nana*. She'd measured me last.

She'd had on her Sunday best—a spring green dress, gold earrings, and black pumps. "My lands, Vilonia, look at you!" She held me at arm's length before enveloping me in a big old squeeze. Her dress smelled like citrus and wildflowers. "You've grown an inch overnight. Let's see how tall you really are."

"Nana, you measured me *last* week." I'd blushed while secretly loving the attention. Having always been small, I never tired of hearing I'd grown.

Undoing the clasp on her black handbag, Nana whipped out a yellow No. 2 pencil.

"You know the drill. Shoes off, heels to the wall, uh-huh. That's good. Chin up, but not too far now."

I obeyed. Nobody crossed Nana.

"I've brought new sheet music," she said, scratching the wall next to my head. "Okay, hon. Turn around." She beamed. "Forty-eight and one-half inches! Would you take a look at that?"

"Impossible!" I traced the mark with my pointer finger.

"Up a quarter of an inch." She stuck the yellow pencil

behind her ear. "And you didn't believe your nana."

I had smiled because she was right and because I'd felt taller already. Maybe I'd land on Dr. Stacy's pediatric growth chart once and for all.

"Now, let's see how you like the music. Come on."

Good heavens, not another hymn. Nana had been in a bit of a rut when it came to gospel music. I could play them all: *Amazing Grace, Blessed Assurance,* even *I'll Fly Away,* which I darn near did.

"You don't know what you're in for, Vilonia baby. A bit of soul does a body good." Nana plopped the music onto the stand, then patted the spot on the bench next to her. I sat, because I knew what was good for me, and because I loved hearing her play.

"You know why I like Ray Charles?" she asked as sweet, bluesy notes swirled around us, filling the empty space.

I shook my head, thinking Ray Charles was the happiest-looking man I'd ever seen. Smart, too, to wear sunglasses while under all those stage lights.

"He lost his baby brother, his sight—yes, he was blind by your age—and then his parents. But he went on to create beautiful music for the world to enjoy. He was a fighter, Vilonia." Nana smiled at me. "Just. Like. You."

Nana's fingers danced across the keys. Mine had flown to the scars on my wrist. *A fighter, huh.* I repeated to myself. I could live with that.

Chapter Six

I didn't answer the phone Saturday morning, Max day two, when Caller ID flashed *Bettina Wiggins*. I knew she wanted that obit, and I couldn't tell her the truth. It wasn't done.

I hadn't written it yet.

Mama had a saying, "If you tell the truth, you don't have to remember anything." The real truth was she stole that quote from author Mark Twain, who probably stole it from Huckleberry Finn. It was a good quote, but I've learned the truth isn't always pretty or fun.

Truth: Forty-five days ago Mama laughed and danced in the kitchen. I did homework (math) at the table. We talked about getting a dog. She stirred her homemade pasta sauce with extra basil and had just preheated the oven to bake a cake. Then the phone rang with news that changed everything.

Nana had collapsed at Boyd's Music & More, right by a display of metronomes. She died clutching her last purchase, a complete songbook of *Ray Charles's Greatest Hits*, to her heart.

Mr. Boyd refunded the book, saying it was his gift to us.

I haven't even opened it. Looking at the glossy cover made me both sad and mad. Sad I'd never see Nana again and mad that she really left.

We braved the memorial as best we could, then Mama crawled under her covers and stayed put. She never could bring herself to write Nana's obit. Waking up in the mornings without your own mama was tough.

I'd know. Not that I thought Mama was feeling sorry for herself or ignoring us on purpose, but when Nana passed, we lost a piece of Mama, too.

Who'd have thought Daddy and I'd be in charge of shopping, meals, laundry, schedules, and a zillion other details, along with my schoolwork and his job. To be fair, Daddy thought Miss Bettina had the obits, and Leon did take on all the yard work and outside chores. So our shrubs were bald, and we ate our way through the frozen food aisle, but we hadn't run out of toilet paper. Yet.

This morning had been interesting enough as the boys had returned early from fishing. The fish weren't biting, so Daddy surprised Mama with a bouquet of sweet-smelling wildflowers. I jammed them into a root beer bottle pulled from the recycling bin, gave them a drink of water, and set them on the table. I'm no florist, but they looked pretty in a haphazard sort of way.

Mama walked in wearing her pajamas. They'd grown so

47

baggy you could fit two Mamas inside. Or maybe Mama had shrunk since she quit cooking. I watched as she poured us all bowls of Rice Crunchies, something she would have frowned on forty-six days ago but now saw as a victory. Daddy and Leon got seconds and thirds respectively, saying it was the best cereal they'd ever eaten. Mama didn't smile, but she did joke she'd handpicked and dried the puffed rice herself. Between her pouring cereal and running to the store for milk, hope sprouted in my heart. Baby steps.

Then something about the word search on the back of the box sent Mama spiraling.

"Even the cereal is taunting me," she wailed, and retreated to her room. Grief was weird.

The three of us sat in silence while our cereal got soggier by the second. Daddy folded his napkin and scooted his bowl to the center of the table. "I was getting full anyway."

On cue, Leon's spoon clattered into his bowl, and he wiped his mouth with the back of his hand. "I couldn't tell her we were out of juice, too."

I smiled. He could be all right sometimes.

Daddy spoke, "I know it's been rough the last several weeks." He paused, plucked a broken wildflower from the bottle, and rolled it between his fingers. "Doctor Fenway believes your mama may be depressed."

"I could have told you that." Leon put his hands behind his head.

"It's murky waters." Daddy shot him a look.

"But how do we know?" I asked. "Is she sad or depressed?"

Daddy rubbed his face with his hands. "It's complicated. People grieve differently, and sometimes depression becomes part of their journey. We don't know for sure what's going on, but we do know your mama needs to be well enough to eat and function. Which is why we're talking to the doctor."

My stomach twisted in knots. "But she'll get better, right?"

Daddy forced a smile. "It's hard, Tadpole, because you can't see it to treat it like you would a rash or a broken arm."

My nose stung, warning I was near tears. "So, what *can* we do?"

"Keep doing what we've been doing. Let her know we love her, and we're still here."

"What about medicine?" I asked. "Or therapy?" Or better yet, I thought, a *therapeutic pet*?

"Yeah. Did he say how long it'd last?" Leon asked. "Nana's been gone, what? Six weeks?"

"Forty-six days." My voice cracked.

Daddy shook his head. "It's a process. Her medicine should help, though it may take a couple weeks. The good news is she's starting to see a counselor. It's a blessing her boss has been so flexible about work."

I gulped. Her boss had been "flexible" thanks to me. Mama and Daddy both believed Miss Bettina was filling in for her, and Miss Bettina believed Mama was still working.

"Just know she's fighting this. We're a team. Your mama and I love you very much."

"I know, Daddy." I tied my napkin into a tight pretzel roll.

"Yeah," Leon agreed.

Daddy's chair squealed across the floor. "Well, I should go check on your mom. You kids carry on."

Leon picked up Daddy's bowl after he'd left, and then to spite me, he stacked both of their dirty dishes on top of mine. "Gee. Thanks."

Brothers.

I cleared the table and sneaked a peek at the back of the Rice Crunchies box. Ah, a Wizard of Oz word search, where the name DOROTHY was highlighted.

Dorothy was Nana's last name and Mama's maiden.

Okay, Universe, you can stop being cruel.

I poured a glass of milk and stirred in a river of chocolate syrup. Mama wouldn't eat, but maybe she'd take a drink. Chocolate made everything better.

I plopped in a swirly straw and knocked on her door.

"Mama? I brought you chocolate milk."

Mama sniffled. "Thanks, dear."

"Are you okay?"

"Yeah, baby. I'm just sad." She took a sip, and milk zipped up the straw.

"I know, Mama. I'm sad too."

At the funeral, people kept saying time heals. I wished time would hurry up.

I fed Max and flopped across my bed with Mama's computer and my ANTHROPOLOGY binder, ready to work. Anything to keep Mama employed and Miss Bettina from showing her face. Dalmatians! Nobody had time for that.

I skimmed Mrs. Tooley's information and wondered if anyone she left behind stayed in bed too. I spent the next half hour writing, rewriting, and taking plenty of stretch breaks. It's a delicate thing, a privilege Mama once said, to write about the deceased. I wanted to get it right.

Obituaries, like stories, used a formula. Only instead of a beginning, middle, and an end, obits had five parts: a statement of death, a short biography of the deceased, a list of survivors (family and friends), funeral or wake specifics, and donations. Donations were monetary gifts made to charities in memory of the deceased.

I did my best to work all the parts in. Whenever I got stuck, I flipped through my binder of obituaries for a sample. It wasn't hard substituting *beloved teacher* for *dog walker*, and so on. But Mrs. Tooley's family had done such a good job supplying information, hers came together smooth as a baby's butt. If only my nana's would too.

"Hey, Max, tell me what you think about this." I cleared my throat and read:

Martha Adele Tooley, 81, of Brandon, MS—beloved wife, accountant, and bosom friend to many—expired peacefully in her sleep on Wednesday, April 15. Tax Day. A wizard with numbers, Martha graduated from Howard County High School in 1951 with high honors. She was promoted quickly from bookkeeper at age twenty to accountant and then to CPA after acing all four parts of the board exam on her first try. (Boom!) She'd be mortified we told you. We'll miss her bubbly laugh, her wild socks, and her homemade lobster mac and cheese (but not her zucchini bread). Martha loved pie but loathed jogging. She adored her playful pugs, Harper and Lee, but had a strong distrust of cats. She often said books balanced her creative right brain from her mathematical left. She was especially proud of her rare Flannery O'Connor collection. Martha leaves behind Richard (Rick) Tooley, her husband of fifty-three years (fifty-two if you ask him); a younger sister, Ruth Braxton of Longview, TX; her two pugs; and a host of friends—every one lucky to have known her.

Funeral services will be held Wednesday, April 22, 2:00 p.m., at St. Stephen's Chapel. The family encourages everyone to wear their wildest socks. In lieu of flowers, please consider donations to the Flannery O'Connor–Andalusia Foundation, Inc. P.O. Box 947, Milledgeville, GA 31059. Or to Hannah's Socks at hannahssocks.org.

Max swam to the other side of his bowl, but I'm saying he gave me two fins up.

I ran spell check, then e-mailed it lickety-split to Miss Bettina. I hoped the family would be pleased, because that's who obituaries were really for. The living.

One look at my binder could tell you that.

Chapter Seven

Spring Break was pretty uneventful.

Sunday, Max day three, was spent at church. Mama got up and dressed in a pretty sleeveless dress with a flowing skirt. She looked like a vision with her hair tied back in a loose knot. Could the science be right? That after only three days of having Max in the house, some kind of magic was happening? Even Daddy wore his nicest shirt and shaved. Daddy only shaved for the big holiday services like Easter, Christmas, and his own wedding. Leon put on a belt and . . . what was that? Spray *cologne*? I ran sputtering from our bathroom, and my obituary flashed in my mind: *Vilonia Renae Beebe departed this world on Sunday, April 19, after being fumigated with cologne by a family member (whose name rhymes with "neon").*

Once my eyes stopped stinging, I chose a T-shirt and my navy blue skirt. I liked this skirt because it had shorts sewn inside. Mama called it a skort. Skirt plus shorts. I said that's the silliest name for a piece of clothing I'd ever heard. My skort looked like a skirt but didn't keep me from sliding into bases or climbing trees, and that's all that mattered to me.

We sneaked into church a few minutes late and sat in the back pew. I spotted Miss Bettina's huge head front and center. She probably records the whole sermon. Pastor finished preaching, and we slipped out during the Lord's Prayer. Good thing, because who knows what would have happened had Miss Bettina cornered Mama about work. Anyway, I think God understood small talk wore Mama out.

After lunch, I radioed Ava Claire on the walkie-talkie she'd given me for my last birthday to see if she wanted to play. She never answered.

On Monday, Max day four, I put on my favorite dog shirt and dropped by the Willoughbys' to check on Eleanor. I shuffled up the walk and spotted Ransom with a garden hose in hand, giving their chocolate Lab, John Quincy Adams, a bath. Rory was there too. He threw me a quick smile and waved. I waved back. Quincy saw me and barked, then bounded out of his bath. He sprinted toward me across the sweet-smelling, fresh-cut grass. His tongue lolled out to one side, so low I worried he'd trip.

Mrs. Willoughby looked up from watering the ferns on her front porch and beamed. "Vilonia! What a nice surprise."

Quincy must have thought so too. He jumped up to lick my face and knocked my cap clean off my head.

"Quincy!" Rory boomed. "Sit."

Quincy sat, his sudsy tail thump-thumping excitedly against the walk as my heart turned to mush. Rory picked up my cap and blushed. "He likes visitors but needs to work on his hello."

Mrs. Willoughby patted the top of Quincy's wet head. "We have time. He's still a pup."

"He's perfect." I knelt down to pet him and plucked a few blades of grass from his coat. *Thump-thump-thump,* his tail beat a steady rhythm. "But he may need another bath."

Quincy's ears twitched at the word "bath." He lay down, put his head between his paws, and whimpered. Everyone laughed. I couldn't help but quote *Winn-Dixie.* "It's hard not to immediately fall in love with a dog who has a good sense of humor."

"Or anyone, for that matter." Mrs. Willoughby laughed. "Ransom, turn off the hose and fetch Eleanor. Vilonia needs to see her, and Rory can handle John Quincy." Turning to me, she bragged about Eleanor's recovery and how she hoped I'd make the festival.

"Mrs. Willoughby, I've been every year since I was a baby. I don't intend to miss now."

"Well, tell your daddy that Tom Sawyer's would be honored if he'd consider frying fish again this year."

"I'll tell him." I grinned proudly. "Nobody fries fish like Daddy." Then, before I left, she gave me a dozen eggs and had Rory bring me a surprise.

He popped inside the house and came back carrying a brown grocery bag.

"It's a thank-you. For saving Eleanor." His cheeks burned pink. "I picked it out."

"True story," Mrs. Willoughby said.

"Thank you," I told them, and peeked inside, bracing myself for a snake to jump out. Instead, there appeared to be a gently used book and boxes upon boxes of sparklers.

"Sparklers are our number one seller," Rory said.

"Also true," added Mrs. Willoughby.

"Nice." I reached inside for the book and gasped. *"Because of Winn-Dixie."* I ran my finger across the title. "It's my favorite."

Rory grinned. "I know. You're always reading the library's copy."

I blushed. "I'll take good care of it. Thank you."

"Thank you, honey, for saving our Ellie. Tell your daddy we'll see him soon."

I spent that night at AC's. It was the first break she'd had from rehearsals. We stayed up too late as usual.

Tuesday morning, Max day five, I headed home bright and early to heat up frozen waffles, since AC had dance rehearsal (again). I revised one obit and made another go at writing Nana's. It wound up in the trash. I then spent my entire afternoon at the public library researching dog ownership, online adoption forms, and skimming through photos of the county's latest rescues. I had to be prepared to state my case if or when one of the Tooley puppies needed a home. Strange I hadn't seen or heard anything yet. I made a mental note to stop by the vet.

Wednesday, Max day six, was an unofficial softball practice day as most of the team had left for vacation. I biked to the field and ran through a series of windmill pitching drills to nail mechanics. Coach and I worked on wrist snaps, half circles, full circles, and exploding off the mound. My arm was tuckered out, but a friendly game of pickup had started amongst my teammates, a couple of older girls, and Ransom and Rory's team. I couldn't shake those Willoughbys for nothing, but I'd never turned a boys-versus-girls game down. It's unconstitutional. Spoiler: We lost, but I managed to strike out Ransom. I knew Rory wouldn't let him forget it either.

That afternoon, I fed Max and gave him a tour of my backyard. I might have played Chopsticks for him a dozen times on the piano. AC was, big surprise, at dance. A postcard came in the mail from my teammate Phoebe with a photograph of the ocean lapping a sandy beach sprinkled with colorful umbrellas. I wondered if my family would ever go on vacation again. Oh, I stopped by Best Friends, but a sign on the door said CLOSED. Weird.

Thursday, Max day seven, it rained the entire day. Max and I had a Harry Potter movie marathon. AC was going to join us, but Neely said her dance instructor took her shopping and out for ice cream. I secretly hoped it was freezer burned.

By Friday, I was going a little loco. Daddy took Leon fishing to get his mind off next week's track tryouts, and Mama made us both PBJs for lunch and then went back to bed. Plus there was still no word on the puppies.

After deleting my and Miss Bettina's last chain of work e-mails, I sighed. The responsible thing would be to give Nana's obituary another go. Nana couldn't stand tardiness, and she'd be madder than a hornet to know we hadn't run hers yet. Most obituaries posted within a couple of days of the deceased's passing. Not forty-something days. And if I didn't hurry, it'd soon be fifty-something. I stretched my arms out the way Coach taught me, cracked my knuckles, and began:

Lola Mae Dorothy, 68, beloved mother and nana, went to her eternal home on Friday, March 4. Born to Forrest and Alice Susan Copeland on

My fingers stopped their typing, and my eyes blurred. *Forget it,* I sniffled. It still stung and felt all raw, like when you fall and skin your palms and have to pluck out itty bits of gravel for days to come.

Poodles. At least I'd tried. Which was more than Mama had done. Maybe it'd be easier if we wrote it together.

I shut Mama's laptop and slid off the bed. Sweeping my hair into an easy ponytail, I looked into the mirror and froze. All this being responsible had got to me. Bad.

"Max, my freckles are gone!" I moved toward the glass and poked at my face. A steady lack of UV rays had wiped my forehead, my cheeks, even my small nose, which somehow usually hosted a galaxy of freckles, clean. "Max, imagine if you woke up one day with no scales. You'd feel naked." And I did. Freckles had been my trademark. My body was experiencing a Vitamin D crisis. I needed sun.

I carried Mama's laptop downstairs and peeked in on her. Still snoozing. I clicked the door shut and set her computer on the coffee table. And because I didn't want to leave Max all alone in my room, I moved him downstairs too. He was used to being around people at the library, and he looked right at home on the piano, next to a stack of magazines.

Sigh. "See you, Max." I tromped across the yard and knocked on the Nutters' door.

"Hey," AC answered. She had on striped leggings, a skirt, and a new glittery shirt that said "Just Dance." Her hair was even piled on top of her head in one of those messy buns. I'd look like a sequin-dipped Q-tip if I tried that stunt.

"Hey back." I tugged at my shrunken baseball tee.

Her eyebrows shot up. "So. How's your dog research coming?"

"Slow. Wanna ride bikes or something? That is, if you don't have dance."

A smile spread across her face. "Danced this morning. Let me ask Neely."

Neely/Mrs. Nutter/Ava Claire's mom worked as a certified nail stylist at the Posh Palace, Howard County's premier (and only) beauty salon. It was safe to say that AC had, hands down, the coolest nails at Howard County Elementary.

AC returned with two green apples. "Hungry?"

"Nah."

She handed me one anyway. "Neely insisted."

"Okay, thanks." I took a bite, secretly thankful for the fresh fruit. It crunched sweet and crisp.

We sat on her front steps and ate until all we had left were cores and sticky fingers.

"Heard from the general?"

AC sighed. "Neely did. The usual. Sends his love. Can't wait to be home."

I nodded, silent.

"Hey, I want to see Max. How's he doing?"

"Fine." I took one last bite.

"What'd your parents say?"

"Dad's cool with it. Mama hasn't said much. To be honest, I'm not sure she's even seen him."

It was AC's turn to grow silent. She plucked a seed from between her teeth and tossed it onto the grass. "See how far you can throw," she said. "I'll go first."

She chucked her apple core across the yard.

I gripped mine in my left hand and threw with all I had. "Softball, AC. It pays to play."

I stood up and took off in a dead run, yelling over my shoulder. "Last one in's a rotten egg!"

We raced from her driveway to mine, laughing the whole way.

"No fair! I'm wearing fancy shoes." AC sprinted up behind me, out of breath and holding a silver sandal in each hand.

"You have fancy shoes on *every* day." I laughed. Even her sneakers were covered in rhinestones.

"True." Her brown eyes sparkled underneath her perfectly trimmed bangs. "Hey, look who's home." She jerked her thumb toward Daddy's shop.

"Yeah. Bet they're cleaning. Let's see what they caught."

AC slipped into her shoes, and we wound our way down the gravel drive to Daddy's shop, a detached single-car garage big enough to house a fishing boat.

"If it isn't Frog and Toad." Dad tipped his fishing cap in a mock salute.

"Hi, Mr. B." AC waved. "Nice hat." She held her nose at the smell of fish, sweat, and bait.

I stood on my tiptoes and peered inside the boat's live well. "How many did you catch?"

"Fourteen. Two brim. Twelve striped bass." Dad reached into the well and pulled out a five-pound bass by its mouth.

"And Leon?" I asked, guessing he had hit the shower.

"Caught half."

I could do as well if not better, but I didn't say a word.

"I'm going in to get a drink of water now," AC piped up. She looked queasy.

I nodded, watching Daddy's tanned arms hoist the cooler filled with ice and fish. He set it on the side of the boat, hopped out, and then carried the chest to his outdoor sink. AC hadn't smelled anything yet. Cleaning fish was messy, stinky work, but I enjoyed sitting on the rusted-out metal stool next to Daddy as he slipped his blade behind the gills and slid it down the fish's sides, removing the bones. Sometimes, he'd point the tip of his knife at the fish's vital organs, naming each one—heart, liver, stomach. Every once in a while, if it was a she, eggs.

"Run in with your friend. You can help clean 'em next time." Dad slapped the first fish on the homemade butcher-block table, its shiny belly toward him, its slimy tail pointing left. The sign of a left-handed fisherman.

Leon's a righty. And Mama and Nana. But Daddy and I, we are lefties through and through.

I pushed the door open into the kitchen. Ava Claire, seated at the dining table with a tall glass of ice water, stopped talking midsentence. Maybe Mama was up.

Wrong.

Miss Bettina was. I watched in horror as she unwrapped the last of Mama's Little Debbie snack cakes. I knew it was the last, because I kept inventory. What I didn't know was how she'd gotten in here, and more important, *why*. I'd sent the obituary. I knew I had.

"Vilonia." She said my name like a teacher asking to see me after class. "I was hoping to find you." She bit into Mama's cake. A chocolate crumb fell onto the table.

"Find me?" I pointed to myself and looked at AC. I knew from her sudden wide eyes and nail chewing—AC never bit her nails—that she had no clue what this meeting was about. That made two of us.

"Yes." Miss Bettina swallowed. She drummed her fat fingers across a manila envelope on the table and pressed her full lips into a tight line. She wasn't one to choose her words. *Great Danes.* This could only mean one thing.

She'd figured out my cover. And after all the work of trying to write in Mama's best, most professional obituary voice . . . I gripped the back of the empty chair. I wouldn't cry. I would not.

Miss Bettina glanced at AC, then back to me. "The puppies," she said.

I released my death grip on the chair. "Yes?" I asked, scooting the chair out and sinking into its seat.

"The puppies have arrived."

Chapter Eight

What puppies?" AC asked.

"Mrs. Tooley's." I reached over and took a sip of her ice water. We were long past the fear of catching each other's germs.

"My sources tell me they were born three days ago." Another bite of cake.

"What? Three whole days?"

"I'm sorry, Vilonia. I've told you everything I know. Now if you'll excuse me, I have to run by work before my ballroom dancing class. It's rumba night." Miss Bettina crumpled the cake wrapper and stood. Her knees popped, and she mumbled something about old age. *Age schmage.* There was no excuse for her not knowing the facts. She ran a newspaper, for schnauzer's sake. It was her job to report noteworthy information.

"But every minute counts!" I blurted. "Someone else could swoop in and adopt one before me."

"Did your parents cave?" AC grabbed my arm and

squealed. "You should have said something. Are you seriously getting a puppy?"

"Shhh." I shook off her arm and stood. AC drew back. I'd hurt her feelings, but I had no time to explain. The puppies were alive and available. "Miss Bettina, exactly how many people have you told about this?"

Miss Bettina tucked the envelope under her arm. "The puppies?" she asked, all innocent. "Oh, I don't know. I see so many people with my job . . . It's impossible to know, really." She waved her hand in the air to show just how fuzzy the numbers were. Ava Claire snorted.

Miss Bettina pushed her thick frames up the bridge of her nose to answer her buzzing phone. Unbelievable. It was probably someone else wanting insider puppy information. My jaw clenched.

Ava Claire carried her glass to the sink and dumped the water out.

"AC, I'm sorry. I'll explain later, okay?"

"Thanks for the water," she said, cool as ice. "Good-bye, Miss B."

"Bye, hon." Miss Bettina paused her conversation. "Thanks for showing me in." *So that's how she got inside.*

The door shut, and I dropped my head. It's bad enough I lost my nana, now I'm losing my mama, quite possibly my maybe dog, and my best friend, too.

Miss Bettina ended her call.

"The paper needs me . . . would you see your mama gets this? It's an out-of-towner." Miss Bettina passed me the slender manila packet before she bulldozed her way across the living room to the front door.

"Sure." I trailed her slowly, turning over the envelope as I walked. One name was scrawled across the front in red ink. *Janet.*

Halfway across the room, Miss Bettina stopped and frowned. "Vilonia. This goldfish has the fungus."

"What?" My heart stopped cold. I dropped the envelope onto the sofa and followed her pointer finger.

"See?" she said, leaning over the glass bowl. "Fungus."

"I don't—Max? *Max!*" I ran to his fishbowl sitting on top of my piano and peered inside. Sure enough, Max had rolled onto his side, his top fin white-coated and flailing. He wasn't floating, but he wasn't swimming. He stared straight ahead.

That's fish for "Help!"

I didn't know fish could even catch fungi. Some fisherman's daughter I was.

"Miss Bettina, I'm terribly sorry, but you'll have to come back another time." I grabbed the strap of her workbag and half dragged her to the door. She stepped outside. I waved good-bye. *Click.* My fingers flicked the dead bolt.

I zipped back and grabbed Max, fishbowl and all. With a backward glance to make sure Mama's door was still closed, I ran out the side door. There was no time to leave a note. This was a matter of life or death.

I set Max in my bike's handlebar basket and sped off. Rounding the corner, I met a rock. Water sloshed out of the fishbowl, but I pressed on. Nothing would happen to Mr. Reyes's fish. No, siree. Not on my watch.

"Hang on, Max. We're almost there."

Turning into the Best Friends Animal Clinic lot, I took the wheelchair access ramp up the walk and squealed to a stop right outside the door.

"Make way," I said to a lady exiting the clinic with a mini pinscher. "I've got a fish-mergency coming through!"

Chapter Nine

Miss Sogbottom hung up the phone. "Not another runaway hen."

"No, Miss Sogbottom. This one's far worse." I plopped Max's fishbowl on the counter. The water splashed inside. I cupped my hand around my mouth and whispered, "It's an attack of *fungi*." I glanced over at Max before adding, "He's really bad off. Do you think the doc can help?"

Miss Sogbottom looked at me and blew a giant bubble from her wad of gum. I watched, mesmerized, as the elastic pink bubble eclipsed first her mouth, then her nose, before finally stopping underneath her purple-lined eyes. I opened my mouth to inquire again about Max, but Miss Sogbottom reached up first and poked one of her long fake fingernails into the balloon of gum. The bubble burst all over her nose. Under different circumstances, I would have laughed. But this fishy situation meant life or death, a tank or a toilet. I think Miss Sogbottom sensed my urgency, because she peeled the gum off her face and dropped it into her mouth with a shrug. "Let's ask."

The receptionist padded down the hall in her scrubs and plastic clogs and stopped midway to make sure I was coming. I picked up Max and followed her into exam room number two.

"Dr. Kieklack will be in shortly."

"Thank you," I said, setting Max's bowl on the exam table. "Before you go, can you tell me about the puppies that were born a few days ago?"

"Puppies?" She tilted her chin.

"I heard Mrs. Tooley's dog had puppies."

Miss Sogbottom frowned. "Oh, right. So sad."

I sucked in a breath and let it out. "You mean about Mrs. Tooley?"

"Well, yes. But Mr. Tooley doesn't want the puppies now that his wife's gone, so we must place them, find them homes, as soon as they've weaned."

"So they're okay? They're alive?" I clasped my hands together while my heart performed somersaults inside my chest. "I heard they were premature."

She squinted at me through her bedazzled glasses. "No, they were term."

Good old Miss Bettina, I thought. She would milk anything for a good story.

"But one *is* smaller than the rest. Mom won't have anything to do with him." Miss Sogbottom shook her head. "He's—"

She glanced into the hall, like maybe she had better things to do than gossip about new pups.

"He's . . . ," I prompted, placing my hands over the top of Max's bowl so he couldn't hear.

"He's pretty sick," she continued. "Dr. Kieklack took him home overnight to feed him and keep a close eye on him." The front door chimed. "Foster care is coming later today. Sometime before closing."

Jack Russells. This did not sound good. I wanted to cry right then and there, but I had to stay strong . . . for Max, of course.

"May I see him?"

A voice snapped from near the front desk. "Hello? Does anyone work here?"

Miss Sogbottom sighed and fiddled with a suddenly annoying earring. It was then I realized her earrings were shaped like tiny paw prints. I knew I liked her. "See me before you go, and good luck with the fish." She turned on her heel and left with her ponytail swinging behind her.

I leaned over and peered into the water. Max didn't look too good. White cotton-looking fluffs stuck to his fins and body. If Dr. Kieklack could help those pups, he could help Max, too.

"Hang in there, Max," I whispered. "Help is on the way."

Help, a.k.a. Dr. Kieklack, appeared. He wore his usual— cowboy boots, a white lab coat with *Best Friends Animal*

Clinic stitched over the chest pocket, and a bow tie. Today's had navy polka dots. I had a lot of respect for Dr. Kieklack. Not only did he mix boots with a bowtie, he knew everything there was to know about animals, from what to give a box turtle with indigestion to helping a Jersey cow calve.

"Hello, Vilonia. Who do you have with you today?"

"This is Max." I stepped aside to give Dr. Kieklack a better look. "He's the library—I mean, he's my pet goldfish." Dr. Kieklack arched an eyebrow. "I won him last week," I added real fast, "and now he's growing white fluff." I pressed my lips together. I hated lying about Max, but Howard County wasn't some bustling metropolis. Everyone knew everybody and word traveled fast. I couldn't risk Mr. Reyes hearing his fish was at the vet.

Dr. Kieklack bent over the fishbowl like one of those bendy straws and nodded. "I see."

"Miss Bettina said he'd caught fungus." I wiped my sweaty palms on my shorts. "I didn't know fish could catch that."

Dr. Kieklack smiled and straightened. "Unfortunately, they can. Especially if they have a fresh wound. Sometimes they can scrape themselves on decorative objects, such as this shell, or even pick up a parasite. But don't be too hard on yourself. It's difficult to see an injury until it gets infected. That's why careful maintenance is important."

"Oh." I frowned, suddenly feeling sick. "Is it, you know, *terminal*? Because if he's on his last fin, you can tell me. My mama writes obits for a living." I sucked in a sharp breath and threw my shoulders back.

"Not usually, no." Dr. Kieklack reached inside a drawer and found a small fishnet.

"Phew!" I smiled.

"However." He held up a hand. "Max's case seems pretty aggressive and advanced. I'm not aware of his environment or circumstances prior to your adopting him, but I'm afraid I can't give you much hope . . ."

"It's okay, Dr. Kieklack, I can take it." I swallowed hard, trying to convince myself. "Tell me what to do to keep him comfortable in his last moments." *That's the least I can do for poor Max and Mr. Reyes.*

Dr. Kieklack brushed his bit of stubble, lost in thought. "Well, there's a scrub, but his system's probably too weak for that. I can send you home with a bottle of Fish Remedy that should treat any infection and promote regrowth of damaged tissue. You can add three drops to his water to start with. It's a long shot, but it may help."

"Thanks." I smiled again, taking the bottle.

"Miss Sogbottom can give you a care sheet up front. It has tips on changing his water, cleaning his bowl, and signs to look for, so hopefully this doesn't happen again. Good luck, Vilonia." Dr. Kieklack pumped my hand. "Be sure to let me know how he does. And best of luck to you, Mr. Max."

Dr. Kieklack bent down and put his hand on the side of

the glass. His brown eyes shined with kindness. I could feel it, and I knew Max could too.

I carried Max and his bill to the front to check out, only to realize I'd left in such a rush, I'd forgotten my pet fund. It was a small miracle I happened to have five dollars and eighteen cents in my pocket. But I still owed twenty more dollars. Talk about embarrassing.

"Don't worry, I'll cover the rest," Miss Sogbottom said.

"Miss Sogbottom, I may be a kid, but I'm no thief. I'll pay you back someday, I promise. Would you prefer cash or cake?"

Miss Sogbottom thought for a second. "Surprise me."

"You got it. I do need one more thing, though. Dr. Kieklack said something about a care sheet?"

"Ah. Here you go." Miss Sogbottom handed me the page and winked. Only when I tried to tug it away from her, she didn't let go. "Why don't you two exit through the *back*? Sometimes UPS blocks the front drive."

When I didn't move, because I was 100 percent confused, she smacked her bubblegum and rolled her eyes. "Come on, follow me."

"Uh, okay," I answered. Never mind that my bike was parked out front and there was no delivery truck.

I carried Max and his instructions through the back of the office, down another long sterile hallway. Dogs, waiting to be groomed or picked up, barked in their kennels on the other side of the wall. My heart beat fast.

Miss Sogbottom stopped outside the last door on the left. The door was open. Dr. Kieklack's office.

"Five minutes. You have five minutes, and not a second more." She pointed to a kennel on the floor. "Look with your eyes, not your hands. Understand?"

I nodded, too excited to speak.

The phone up front rang, and she flinched.

"No touching," I said, finding my voice. "Got it."

She gave me two thumbs up and scurried to answer the phone. I left Max on a wooden chair by the door and crept into the room. It was a tiny office. And dark. Dr. Kieklack's desk took up most of the space. With the overhead lights switched off and the shade drawn, his desk lamp cast the only soft light about the room. Dr. K probably wanted it that way, all cozy and quiet for the puppy.

I stepped close enough to peek inside the crate but chickened out, squeezing my eyes shut at the last second. *Kibbles 'n Bits,* I was turning into a sissy.

Honest to goodness, though, I'd pumped my puppy expectations so high, I wasn't sure I could handle the reality of this runt. Or worse, what if I could? What if I looked at his sweet face and fell head-over-heels in real-deal puppy love, only to learn I was completely, hopelessly in way over my head?

Oh well. It wouldn't be the first time.

Chapter Ten

My eyes flew open, and a giant "Awww" escaped my mouth. Of course no one was in the room to awww with me. It was just impossible to look at this tiny black muzzle and *not* say it.

This pup was an explosion of cute. With his sandy fur and teensy black ears, my heart expanded one puppy size.

Okay, he looked more like an itty-bitty sleeping guinea pig than a pug. A tan guinea pig with silky fur, a wrinkly forehead, and the sweetest pink heart-shaped nose. He yawned. I died of cute.

"You are the best thing ever. Look at you all snuggled up to your blanket."

He grunted, but I knew he couldn't hear or see me. According to my extensive research, puppies are born deaf, blind, and toothless (talk about a rough start) and stay that way until they reach two weeks old. They rely on their mamas for everything— food, baths, and warmth.

"But you, little guy, you're on your own. Thank God for Dr. Kieklack, huh?"

I noted the tray of feeding syringes and formula on the veterinarian's desk, as well as the cord running from the kennel to the outlet in the wall. I'd bet a dollar there was a heating pad under the puppy's bed. A makeshift incubator. Being chilled was the leading cause of death in puppies—one obit I wouldn't want to write.

His soft sides moved in and out with each shaky breath. One. Two. Three. Pause. I counted each breath like I had the power to keep him breathing. Nana said they'd done the same when I was in the NICU.

"You're a fighter, you know," I whispered. "Do you have a name? Because if you don't, I'll give you one. I'm good with names. I'm Vilonia, by the way."

His front paw twitched.

Footsteps echoed in the hall. My five minutes had vanished. I glanced once more at the puppy that had experienced a lifetime of heartache in his first day of life. And that's when his name came to me.

"Good-bye, Ray Charles. I like you already."

I carried Max through the back door and into the warm sunlight, thanking him for his patience. That was the great thing about fish. They're excellent waiters.

"See this sheet, Max?" I asked, holding his care sheet to the glass. "I'm going to follow these tips precisely. We'll get you better in no time." I sat Max back inside my handlebar's basket and could have sworn over Mrs. Tooley's dead body (may she rest in peace) that Max looked at me and winked.

That's fish for "Thanks."

Chapter Eleven

I pedaled as fast as I dared toward home without upsetting the fishbowl. Turning onto my street, I met Ava Claire riding toward me on her bike with handlebar streamers.

"Whatcha doing?" she asked, screeching her bike to a stop. "Or are you too busy to talk?"

Ouch. AC still acted hurt, but she couldn't stay mad at me. Our history proved it. Besides, she could never pass up drama.

"Something urgent!" I hollered over my shoulder as I bounced into my drive.

"Like *urgent* urgent?" she asked, wheeling her bike around after me. I parked mine and hopped off, carefully easing the kickstand into place.

"Afraid so." I cradled Max's bowl in my hands and let her peer in, then dropped my voice to a whisper. "You can't tell a soul."

"Mr. Reyes's fish! Is he . . . ?" Her face grew pale underneath her glittering purple bike helmet. "Now your mama will never, ever let you get a dog."

"Shut your mouth. He's not dead . . . yet." I swallowed. "I took him to Dr. Kieklack and got some drops, but it doesn't look good."

Ava Claire unbuckled her helmet, and the two of us stood there for a full minute staring deep into the fishbowl, half struck with grief over Max's demise and half frozen in terror knowing I might kill the library pet. I looked my best friend since forever in the face and in my most serious voice said, "This stays between us."

"Cross my heart."

"Hope to, uh, never mind." I cleared my throat. "Can you get the door?"

I brushed past Ava Claire in her twirly skirt, sparkling shoes, and brave pageant smile.

"Now what?" she asked. The door slammed shut behind her.

"Vilonia?" Mama's voice floated into the kitchen.

"Well, *now*, I've got to check on Mama." I shot Ava Claire a thank-you-very-much look and motioned for her to be quiet.

"Sorry," she said with a wince.

"Coming, Mama!" I yelled. I set Max on the kitchen table and quickly added one, two, three drops of Dr. Kieklack's Fish Remedy to his water. "That should do it."

"Do what?" AC asked.

"Remedy the fish."

"Right."

"Here," I said, going to the fridge. "Have some of my world-famous strawberry-infused iced tea while we wait. Made it myself this morning. I even removed the stems this time."

"Gee, thanks." Ava Claire found a seat at the table and smoothed out her skirt. I poured Mama a glass.

"Don't take your eyes off Max. I'll be right back."

Ava Claire was one of the few people in town (other than immediate family) who knew the Truth. And by Truth I mean Mama's delicate condition.

I stole down the wooden floorboards to my parents' bedroom and rap-tap-tapped softly on the door. "Mama?"

"Come in, sweetie."

I pushed the door open and breathed a sigh of relief. Today was a good day. Someone had tied back the curtains, allowing light to stream into the white painted space and chase the shadows away, and Mama, propped up in bed in her paisley pajamas, balanced her computer on a pillow in her lap. She was swimming in newspaper clippings and yellow legal pads with a look of concentration on her face. A pencil was tucked behind her ear.

"You working today, Mama?" I set her glass of tea on the bedside table.

"I can't concentrate." She patted the edge of her soft white duvet, inviting me to come and sit down. "These obits are killing me." She closed her laptop, half smiling at her joke. "But I always have time for you."

I moved a stack of papers and sat next to her, trying to rein

81

in the hope welling in my chest. When was the last time I'd heard her laugh? Crack a joke? I couldn't remember.

"Miss Bettina stopped over."

"I don't blame her." Mama sighed.

"That's so great of her to cover for you until you feel up to working again." I tried to sound confident when I lied. The truth was Miss Bettina thought Mama *was* working.

Mama drew a big breath and bit her lip. "It's been seven weeks, and I still haven't written my own mother's obituary."

"You know, I could help. We could write it together."

Mama patted my leg. "I'm not feeling very brave today, kiddo. Not feeling much of anything. But soon."

She shuffled some of the newspaper clippings into a neat stack.

"Hey. Brought you my world-famous strawberry tea."

She eyed it with suspicion. "Stems?"

"None."

"Hmm." She smiled, took a sip, and then tucked my bangs—which were taking longer than Christmas to grow out—behind my ear. "Delicious. How's your fish?"

"Oh. Max? You saw him?"

"Your daddy showed me."

"He's . . . good."

"That's nice." She patted my leg again. "You know what, Vilonia? I'm ready to be out of this slump." Mama leaned her head back on her headboard and closed her eyes.

Was it possible that after one week, Max's presence had helped? That library book did say fish watching could reduce anxiety and stress. In a flash, I imagined how much happier our home could be if we adopted a cuddly puppy. The question burned on the tip of my tongue.

"That's great, Mama," I said, leaning over to plant a kiss on her warm cheek. "I believe in you."

She looked up at me with those warm chocolatey eyes of hers and whispered, "And I believe in you. Now, skedaddle. All this talking has made me sleepy."

I slipped out of her room and found Ava Claire, nose pressed against the bowl, making fish faces at Max.

My heart stopped. "How is he?"

"He's pretty still."

I squeezed my eyes shut. "Poodles!"

AC fished a strawberry from her tea and kept on, "You do know there's this school rumor that Max is really the seventh or the eleventh goldfish, but Mr. Reyes keeps naming every fish the same."

"Yeah," I whispered, but it didn't make any difference to me. I needed *this* fish to live. This Max was proof that I was responsible, capable of following through. Otherwise, Mr. Reyes had every right to remove my name from the Library Helper board. And worse, my parents would never agree to a dog.

"Hey, he made a flip turn. Maybe he's bouncing back." AC tugged on my arm. I sank into a chair.

"Maybe Dr. Kieklack's drops were just what the vet ordered."

Ava Claire reached for the pitcher of strawberry tea and poured me a glass.

"To Max," I said.

"To Max. Pinkies out."

We clinked our mini Mason jars of crystal-pink liquid together and drank up.

I did, anyway. Ava Claire politely sipped hers like we were at high tea with the queen of England. Wiping off my tea mustache, I plopped my empty jar on the table with a thud right next to the fishbowl.

"Maximus Tropicana," I said. "I believe in you, too."

Chapter Twelve

Ava Claire checked the time on the oven clock. "Oh, shoot. I've got to meet Neely." She clicked her thumbs against her fingernails. "I'm trading in these kittens for glitter."

Ava Claire was the only fourth grader I knew who had a standing nail appointment every Friday afternoon.

"We'll be okay, AC. If his condition changes, I'll find you."

"A girl can never have enough glitter, Vilonia, especially for a major life event. One of these days, I'll convince you to come to the Posh Palace with me."

"Ha!" I about spewed tea across the room. "Not on your life, Ava Claire Nutter. My boring nails are just fine, thank you very much."

"Okay, but if you ever change your mind, you know who to call." Then she leaned across the table and whispered, "But know this. If a big tip comes in, Neely orders vanilla malts from Guy's Pies and Shakes next door."

A smile inched across my face. Ava Claire knew the way to my heart.

"Thanks for the lovely tea, darling. Toodles," she said as she slipped out, careful to guide the door shut. Alone with Max, I picked up the care sheet and studied my naked fingernails for a moment. Short, clean, boring. The perfect length for pitching and typing.

I skimmed the sheet until my eyes found a bold section called *Signs of a Healthy Fish*. Based on the signs listed—healthy appetite, clear eyes, active swimming, regular breathing—Max's health stunk. I kept on reading until I reached *Common Health Issues*.

"Here goes nothing, Max," I read aloud. "Common Health Issues. Fungus." I glanced over at the bowl. I think Max was ignoring me, but I couldn't be sure. I kept reading anyway. This information concerned him. He had a right to know. It's not like he could read it himself. "Symptoms of fungus. White cottonlike patches appear on your fish's body or fins. Check. Loss of appetite. Check. Labored breathing. Uh . . ."

Max gave me one fin up.

"Check. Suggested action." I looked over the top of the page at Max. "This is where we figure out how to fix you, so listen up."

Max stayed quiet. I took that as my cue to keep reading.

"'Test and improve water quality.' Hmm. That's got to be what Dr. Kieklack meant by using these drops to restore the water balance. See? They're already improving your water quality." The sheet then explained how to change out Max's water regularly to keep his habitat (a fancy word for home) clean. Free from disease. Yikes.

A sick feeling sank in my stomach like a piece of gravel dropping to the bottom of Max's bowl. What if this—Max's disease—was my fault? Mr. Reyes said he changed the water before sending Max with me. I skimmed the page some more. Uh-oh. There was a warning about using decorative objects that weren't aquarium approved. Maybe . . . the conch stressed him out, or he cut himself on its rough edge. Dr. Kieklack said that could happen. Or, what if the shell introduced a harmful parasite?

I sighed and rested my head on the table for a good view of Max. He'd looked so perfect and happy riding home on the bus days ago. Not a white patch anywhere. Maybe he'd been sick for a while, and it took this long to show. The clock on the wall ticked away the seconds. Our refrigerator hummed. I yawned. I guess the stress of the morning had done me in.

"No offense, Max," I said, even though he couldn't possibly know my thoughts.

But I need not have even worried. Max couldn't hear me.

Max was dead.

Chapter Thirteen

Dead. Gone. Finished.

Max's little fishy body floated belly-up and still. I hunched over his bowl, tears springing to the corners of my eyes.

"Oh, Max." My voice caught. "I'm sorry. I tried. I really, *really* tried. You'll have the best fish memorial there ever was. Promise."

I opened the cabinet and found a teacup with delicate poppies painted inside its rim. We only used it for holidays or special occasions anyway, say when the preacher and his wife visited (which hasn't happened in a while because of the skunks). I scooped Max into the cup and set him on the kitchen counter while I tried to figure out what to do with him.

What do you do with your librarian's dead pet fish? Oh gosh. Oh gosh. I couldn't think. I mean I could, but it was only about how dead *I'd* be on Monday when I showed up to school with an empty fishbowl. What would I tell Mr. Reyes?

What would I tell my friends? My dad? How was I ever going to get a dog if I couldn't take care of a fish? *One thing at a time, Vi. Breathe.*

I leaned against the counter and did just that. I took a deep breath.

Most people flush their dearly departed fish. But that didn't seem right. Max was no ordinary fish. He belonged to Mr. Reyes. He belonged to the library. He belonged to all of us, in a sense. And he deserved a better send-off than a trip down the toilet.

I pulled out Mama's kitchen junk drawer—the drawer where keys without locks, pens without caps, and packs of Juicy Fruit resided. Looking for something, anything that'd work as a suitable casket for Max. Then I saw it. A toothpick box. I shook the remaining 127 toothpicks (or so it seemed) out into the drawer. I carefully lined the tiny box with a bit of paper towel before placing Max inside. Now, most people at this point would bury him.

I'm not most people.

First, I needed to prepare a eulogy for the service. I sat his bowl in the sink, because I couldn't bear to look at it any longer, as empty as it was. I carried Max in the toothpick box up the stairs to my bedroom. I fished a notebook out from under my bed and found a fresh page. Sitting at my desk, I scribbled today's date, April 22, across the top of the page in orange ink. Max's color. I skipped a space before writing *MAXIMUS*

TROPICANA in capital letters. I drew a double line under his name for good measure, then scrawled underneath that: *A Eulogy by Vilonia Renae Beebe, age 9 3/4.*

Max's tribute came fast and out of nowhere, much like his death. To fill up the white space at the bottom of the page, I drew a picture of Max inside a giant heart bubble. It just seemed right.

I set my orange pen down, and at that exact moment it sunk in what I'd done. I don't mean writing my first eulogy. Nope, I'm talking about the heinous, though unintentional, crime I'd committed: I, Vilonia Renae Beebe, Library Helper and entrusted pet sitter, killed Mr. Reyes's fish.

I jumped up from the desk, my brain reeling. I paced back and forth from my bedroom door to the window overlooking AC's house and back again, my hands clasped over my mouth and my mind screaming one word. *Help!*

My room grew stuffier by the minute. I opened the window. Picking up my walkie-talkie, I propped my elbows on the windowsill and held down the talk button.

"AC, are you there? Over?" Maybe she hadn't left for her nail appointment.

Silence.

"*Nine-one-one*, Ava Claire Nutter! Code red. I repeat, *code red.*" Code red was our term for very important matters that required immediate action, like the time Ava Claire spilled a bottle of Big

Apple Red nail polish on her mom's ivory sofa. Thank heavens for the invention of rubbing alcohol and reversible cushions.

"Forget it," I said, and flung the walkie-talkie onto my bed instead of putting it back on my nightstand where it belonged. I grabbed a striped pillow and flopped myself across the bed as well. I needed to do something with Max, but it didn't seem right to be the sole witness and person performing his memorial service. But I sure wasn't going to waltz into class fishless on Monday morning and write my real answer to the "What I Did Over My Spring Break" essay.

"VB, you copy?" The walkie-talkie crackled.

"Copy. AC, is that you? Over."

"No, it's your fairy godmother here to grant your wildest wish." Giggles floated over the airwaves. I walked over to my window, the window that faced Ava Claire's room. That was the whole reason I let Leon have the bigger room, so I could have the window that faced my new friend's. "Roger, Vilonia. It's me." AC's curtains fluttered and she waved behind the glass. "How's the patient?"

"Um. Remember Mrs. Tooley?"

Ava Claire and I looked at each other through glass panes for a solid minute before she piped up, "I'll be right over."

"Roger that," I said, and placed the walkie-talkie where it belonged on my nightstand next to a tower of books.

With a gentle *rap-tap* on my door, AC poked her face through the crack.

"Can I come in?"

"Sure."

"So. Where's Max?" she asked as gingerly as she could.

My shoulders fell. "On my desk. In the toothpick box."

AC shot me a quizzical look.

"Don't ask."

"Okay . . . what are you going to do with him now?"

"I'm not sure."

"What about Mr. Reyes?"

"I don't know!" I threw my hands up. "I don't know! What am I going to do? I killed the library fish! Do you know what this means? Not only will I be ridiculed at school for the rest of my *days*, I'll lose any chance of adopting Ray Charles!"

Ava Claire's eyes grew wide. "Are you having a nervous breakdown? Because if you are, I can call Neely. She does Dr. Menlow's nails, and she specializes in child psychiatry. Remember how Trent Spacey started plucking his eyelashes out one by one after his parents' divorce? He doesn't—"

"Stop. I do not need a psychiatrist, AC. What I *need* is a goldfish!"

Ava Claire glanced at me and then Max. "Preferably a live one."

I flopped onto my bed and groaned.

"Well?" Ava Claire clicked her nails together. "Are you ready?"

"I am not getting a manicure." I peeked at her from under my pillow.

"Don't be silly," AC said. "What I meant was are you ready for some shopping?"

I sat up and flung my pillow aside. "Ava Claire Nutter, sometimes I underestimate your brilliance. Do you think your mom would drive us to the pet store?"

"Are you kidding me? Does Neely ever pass up a trip to the mall?"

And that's how I let my best friend and next-door neighbor talk me into the most pathetic shopping experience of my life.

Chapter Fourteen

Before I could leave, there were a few things I had to do. Number one, I had to move Max's fishbowl, water drops, and care sheet from the kitchen to my room. I couldn't leave the empty bowl out and give anyone reason to think something was wrong. And secondly, I had to tack a KEEP OUT!!! sign to my bedroom door, complete with extra exclamation points for emphasis. The last thing I needed was peon Leon snooping around and noticing what, or who, had gone missing.

To be safe, I reached inside my desk for my bag of Swedish fish.

"That's your emergency homework stash," Ava Claire said as I tore the plastic packaging with my teeth.

"I know it's hard to believe, but some things are worse than fractions." I spit out a piece of plastic. "Here, go fish."

AC chose one of the red gummies, and I slid the fishbowl closer to the window where it belonged. She gave me the honor of plopping Max's decoy into the water. The fish drifted to the bottom.

"Styled like a pro," AC said, popping a fish into her mouth.

"Thanks." I sighed, plucking my own piece of candy from the bag. "At least if anyone pokes his head into my room, everything looks normal." We chewed our gummies in silence.

"I should run home to make sure Neely's free," AC said.

"Good idea," I said. "I'll come over as soon as I do something with Max."

"Deal."

"Deal."

All alone, I considered tucking Max inside my desk drawer until his memorial, but then thought better of it. I wasn't up-to-date on the decomposition rate of fish, and what if he started to stink? I wrinkled my nose. Daddy stored his catch in the freezer. That's where Max belonged.

So I carried his scaly little body in his makeshift casket down the stairs into the kitchen. Digging elbows deep into the freezer to hide a dubious toothpick box wasn't easy. My fingers stung and turned numb. Three pounds of rock-hard pork butt slipped and clocked me in the cheek. But I did it. I planted him in the way back, behind the lamb chops we never ate on Easter (our first without Nana) and the Creamsicle pops.

"You be good, Max. Don't go anywhere, you hear?" So help me. I'd grown used to talking to him.

I shut the door, picked up all 127 of the toothpicks I'd

spilled, and set them in a little jar. Mama's car keys were gone from their hook on the wall, and on the chalkboard she'd left a note under Daddy's hand-drawn weather forecast of partly cloudy.

Gone to store for bananas. What's with all the toothpicks? XO, Mama

Hmm. I'd have to come up with something to explain the toothpicks, but I was glad to see Mama had gotten up and left the house.

I picked up a piece of chalk:

Gone to mall with AC. Be back soon. —V

And just to drive home how thoughtful and responsible I was, I scribbled a quick *P.S. Cleaned up the toothpicks.*

While my mama drove a sensible blue minivan, Neely, I mean Mrs. Nutter, drove a flashy pink Cadillac. She parked the sleek beast (barely bumping the curb) and made a show of stepping out in her red pumps, garden party dress, and huge round sunglasses.

"Okay, girls," her mouth, lined perfectly in cherry-red lipstick, exclaimed. Mrs. Nutter slid her numerous metallic bangles up her wrist to better see the time on her rhinestone-studded wristwatch. "It's two o'clock. Let's meet in one hour at the food court."

"Got it," Ava Claire and I spoke in unison.

"Okay, then. Behave yourselves. Don't spend all your

money in one place. Stick together. And, Ava Claire darling, remember what you learned at self-defense class about stranger danger."

"Yes, Mom. Be aware, take care."

"Toodles!" Ava Claire's mom said with a wave of her fingers as she bustled away.

Ava Claire and I ran the opposite direction. We rode the escalator up to the second level before walking to the far end of the mall to Pete's Pets.

"Aw, look at the kittens!" Ava Claire spotted them first and sprinted up to the window. I was right behind her but didn't have as good a look at the kittens, as a little boy about four years old and his mother were blocking my view.

"No, Mommy. I want the striped one! Like a tiger."

"Mommy said, 'no pets.' We're going home now."

"No!" The boy wriggled free and planted himself on the cold mall floor. He hugged his chest and turned his chubby little face into a pirate scowl. "I won't go. You can't make me."

"That's it, Tucker. We're leaving." The mom sighed, picked her son up off the floor, and hauled him away screaming, legs flailing, and arms reaching for the kitty he couldn't have.

I thought of Ray Charles and his pink button nose. "I'm kicking too, buddy. On the inside."

AC smiled. "The striped one is cute." We watched the kitten as she lazily licked her front paw, while her brother or sister, more orange in color, batted a toy mouse.

"Come on," I said. "Let's go fish." My sneakers squeaked along the newly buffed floor. Animal smells filled the air.

"Good afternoon, girls. May I help you find something?" a guy with an Afro greeted us from behind the counter. He wore jeans, a blue polo, and a snake, wound around his neck like a scarf. His company name badge read PETE, CHIEF PET EXPERT. Next to his name, someone had doodled a dinosaur in green highlighter.

"Maybe. Give us a second to look," I replied.

"Not a problem," he said, absentmindedly brushing his goatee as he flipped through a catalog with pictures of cats in costumes. "Let me know if you need any help."

"M'kay," I mumbled.

Ava Claire giggled. "I hope he puts the snake back first."

We wandered past the turtles, bearded dragons basking on a log, and one empty ball python terrarium (shudder), to small mammals. There were gray ferrets with pink triangle noses, roly-poly guinea pigs (with their own assortment of dress-up clothes), a few hamsters (one running on his wheel), and dozens of white, red-eyed mice. There were several *ooh*s and *aah*s and *look, how cute* squeals before we arrived at the far side of the shop where a FISH sign dangled from the ceiling. We stared at the wall of aquariums, unsure where to start.

"Who knew there were so many kinds of fish?" Ava Claire asked.

"Seriously," I said, gazing at the aquariums three rows

high. "I don't see any goldfish, do you? Maybe we should ask Pete for help."

Ava Claire covered her mouth, lost in thought. "Vilonia." She motioned for me to come over to the far end of the row. "You don't see any goldfish because there aren't any. Look." She pointed to a giant tank containing multicolored gravel and waving plants. But no fish. Not one.

"What?" I whispered. My eyes searched the label. *Goldfish— blah blah.* Something in me snapped.

"Excuse me!" I marched straight up to the counter. My shoes squealed with each step, but I didn't care. Sheer panic drove me on. "Excuse me!" I repeated louder. "Where are your goldfish? I need a goldfish. It's urgent."

Pete looked up at me and brushed his whiskers again. "Sorry to say I don't have any. But a shipment's coming on Tuesday."

The room began to grow dark. I was losing it. My messy braids grazed the tops of my shoulders as I shook my head. "You don't understand. Tuesday will definitely *not* work. Monday will not work. It has to be this weekend. Can you get me a fish by tomorrow? I'll pay double. Are you into baseball cards? If you are, we could work out a deal."

Ava Claire tugged on my sleeve. "Vi—let it go."

Pete looked completely bewildered.

"I've got to have a fish. I need a fish."

AC smiled. "Can you tell us what happened to the fish?"

Pete shrugged. "Sure. A man came in and bought the whole lot for the Catfish Festival. Said he was going to raffle them off or something."

"Okay, thank you." AC smiled apologetically and dragged me out of the store. Past the reptiles, past the dog treats, past the cute kittens in the window and the store's big bulletin board.

Stop.

I jerked back. Something on the bulletin board had caught my eye. AC groaned, but I ignored her and walked up to the flyer. Up to the photograph of the familiar face. A wrinkly new face connected to two black ears and a heart-shaped nose. I scanned the ad.

FOR ADOPTION
Name: Izzy
Breed: Pug
Gender: Male
Color: Fawn
Age: One week
Sweet disposition. For more information, take a phone number below.

Ray Charles.

If hearts had hunger pangs, then mine starved something awful. I reached out to take a number, and my heart dropped into my stomach. Four numbers were already torn off. Gone.

Four people were walking around with Ray Charles's ripped-off number in their pockets. Four people were aiming to bring him home. All of a sudden, I felt like I'd caught a raging case of poison ivy from the top of my head to between my toes. I took the entire flyer.

On cue, my throat began to close and tears welled up in my eyes. AC planted her hands on my shoulders and looked me square in the face.

"How about I buy you a vanilla malt? It's not Guy's, but it's food. We will come up with a plan, promise."

"Whipped cream on top," I said, letting her lead me away for once. But not before I glanced back inside the shop and saw Pete, Chief Pet Expert, scratching his chin and watching us.

Chapter Fifteen

We slurped down our malts and Neely took the long way home, past the fairgrounds. From the looks of it, every business owner downtown had shuttered his or her shop to help decorate for the Forty-Seventh Annual Catfish Festival. There were tents to put up, booths to open, twinkle lights to string. A hot dog truck roared behind us and turned into the gravel lot.

AC grabbed my arm and squeezed. The carnival rides loomed in the back, filled with ghost passengers. My toes tingled. Just thinking about taking the Ferris wheel to the tip-top made me forget about my troubles for a moment. Two workers were tying balloons to a metal archway that'd serve as the starting line for the Catfish 5k. Of course, Leon planned to run.

"Look, Vilonia!" AC squealed, and dug her fingers into my arm. She pressed her nose against the car window, making it hard for me to see the source of her excitement, even though I'd bet my best glove I knew exactly what it was: the stage.

"You might want to turn here, Mrs. Nutter," I said as AC practically gave herself whiplash to see better. Neely made a right, and sure enough, past the balloon arch, in the eye of the fair, stood the stage where the new Miss Catfish would be crowned. Jasmine Washington won last year, and her royal sixteen-by-twenty portrait still hung on the wall in a fancy gilt frame at her daddy's BBQ joint, right above the tray of tangy-sweet sauces.

"I can't wait to see who will be the new Miss Catfish. Miss Connelly would be so perfect. She made second runner-up last year." AC slumped back into her seat, lost in thought.

"Well, if I had anything to do with it, the crown wouldn't go to DeeAnne Druxbury's big sister. She steals kindergartners' snacks when no one's looking and exercises her toes."

We rolled on past the trailers, looking for Tom Sawyer's yellow food truck. Daddy was there, helping set up picnic tables and chairs, a blue dish towel slung over his shoulder. Neely honked. He looked up, and his face split open with that wide grin of his. Poodles. Why couldn't he agree to a dog?

The whole ride home, Ray Charles's adoption flyer burned a hole in my pocket, reminding me that someone, or some-ones, wanted him too.

Needing a distraction, I invited Ava Claire over for the rest of the afternoon, and thankfully, her mother agreed on the condition we didn't waste the day away watching trashy TV. I told her not to worry. We had important business to attend to, and by business, I meant burial.

We climbed out of the pink Cadillac and, still on a sugar high from the vanilla malts, raced into the house and up the stairs. Only, Ava Claire, two steps ahead of me, stopped at the landing and froze.

"What?" I asked, then looked down the hall. My bedroom door stood wide open, and inside, Leon had parked his sweaty self on top of my little white desk and was biting into an orange Creamsicle.

"What are you doing in my room?" I ripped the KEEP OUT!!! sign off the door and waved it in front of his face. "Hello? Did you read the sign?"

Ava Claire reached for my wrist, but I shook her off, primed for a fight.

Leon pointed his Creamsicle at me. "I think the real question is why are *you* keeping Mr. Reyes's fish in our *freezer*."

"Keep your voice down," I snapped. My fingers pressed against my temples. With a fish to bury, I didn't have time for a headache the size of L-e-o-n. "I can explain. But you can't explain snooping."

"Calm down. I didn't snoop. I grabbed a Creamsicle. Since when is that a crime?"

"Since you made it one by getting involved in none-of-your-business."

"Did you really put Max inside a Creamsicle box?" AC asked.

"No." I flopped onto my fuzzy beanbag. "Behind it."

"Presto." Leon reached behind him and placed the opened toothpick box on my yellow comforter.

I groaned. My life was spinning out of control, like that dizzying teacup ride at the festival.

Leon licked the juice from his Creamsicle before it dripped onto my braided rug. "So, what's your plan? Are you going to tell Dad?" he asked, then slurped the last frozen bite into his mouth.

"No way. I'm trying to be *more* responsible, not less." I pulled my knees up under my chin. "If Dad finds out, my entire dog campaign backfires. Ugh. No way. *No* one can know about this."

Leon smirked and launched the wooden Creamsicle stick across the room. It pinged into the metal trash can by my door. "And he scores!"

"I mean it, Leon." I glared at him. "Ava Claire, please fill Leon in on the master plan. Which he will not repeat to anyone if he knows what's good for him." I could get used to giving commands.

"Here's the deal," AC said, tightening the sophisticated knot of hair on top of her head. "We're looking for a replacement."

Leon snorted. "That's easy. Go to the pet shop."

"Yeah, except the pet shop's sold out," I said.

"What?"

"Seriously." AC put a hand on her hip. "They're all bought

out as prizes for the festival, but I'm sure I could convince Neely to take us back to the mall when the shipment comes in." She paused to inspect a minute chip in her fingernail polish.

"But he said that wouldn't be until Tuesday . . . I have to have a fish by Monday, eight a.m." I thumped my gel pen against the notebook and tried not to wail. "Maybe if we all go to the festival and try to win one . . ."

"Say you win a fish," Leon said. "You've got to make sure it looks like Max. I mean, it needs to be the same size, have the same coloring."

My pen stopped. "I may be a fish killer, but I'm not a total doofus."

"Did I say you were?"

"He's only trying to help," AC interrupted.

I rolled my eyes. Since when did she start sticking up for him?

"And you still have to do something with the body."

"Don't be so morbid, Leon." I shot him a look.

He held his palms up in defense. "Hey, I'm not the one hiding bodies in the back of the freezer."

"Come on, you two." Ava Claire snapped her fingers. "We've got to work together if we're going to pull this off."

"She's right." I frowned, and as much as I didn't want to admit it, I needed Leon's help. "Three heads *are* better than two . . ." I drew circles in my notebook. "What do you think, Leon? We

106

could look online to see who's selling or giving away goldfish."

"No thanks," Leon said. "I don't know about you, but I'm not going to some stranger's home to become fish food."

Ava Claire winced. "Can we stop all the dead-body talk?"

"Sorry." Leon grinned.

I chewed the end of my pen, riddling it with bite marks. "YOU GUYS. What am I going to do? I have to take a fish to school in three days." I hugged my notebook to my middle and paced about the room, following the woven lines of my braided area rug.

"Just stop." Ava Claire clamped her hands firmly on my shoulders and shook me gently. "Worrying won't do you any good. You will get through this, you hear? It may take a mani and pedi and a slice of Guy's banana cream pie, but you will live." AC's eyes stared straight into me. Her voice was steady, strong. "All you can do tonight is bury Max."

"Bury Max," I repeated, pulling away. "Let's bury Max in the creek."

"What?"

"Yeah, what?" AC asked. "You know I don't like it down there. Snapping turtles and snakes and even more snakes." She shuddered.

"Here's what I'm thinking. Leon, remember last fall we watched that show on Vikings and Norsemen?"

Leon nodded. AC stared at us blankly. I went on, "I think Max needs a traditional Norse pyro-funeral."

AC frowned. "'Pyro' as in fire?"

"Yup," I said. "We'll set fire to his box and send him down the creek in a blaze of glory to his final resting place. It's the least we can do."

"I don't know. You can be so dramatic at times." Ava Claire sighed.

I turned to Leon. As his sister, I knew him best. He'd either go one of two ways, all in or be a total bully about it. "Well?"

Leon leaned over his tennis shoes, picking bits of rubber from the toe. No response.

"Leon?"

My older brother looked up at me dead serious and said, "I won't rat you out as a fish killer if you tell me where Dad stashed the Willoughbys' sparklers."

I thought about it for a full two seconds. "You got yourself a deal."

Chapter Sixteen

An hour later, we'd gobbled down dinner and cleared away the dishes. Cooking pasta had plumb wore Mama out. She'd gone to her room with a cup of tea, a sliver of thawed pound cake (because *someone* had stolen the last Little Debbie), and good intentions to write. Daddy kissed Mama good night, then went to his shop to make lures. Turns out, Leon, AC, and I made a great kitchen team. I scrubbed the pots and pans, AC dried them, and Leon put them away. Not where Mama stored them, but good enough. We had things to do, top secret things.

"You should spend the night."

Ava Claire bit her lip. "I don't know. I need to get some sleep. The pageant's tomorrow."

"Don't be ridiculous. All we're doing is laying a fish to rest," I said, wrapping up the leftover cake. "Then we'll go straight to bed. And I know you. You've hung your costume by the door, packed your dance bag, and triple-checked for every hairpin and accessory you'd possibly need."

A smile spread across her face. "Okay."

While Ava Claire called Neely for permission to sleep over, I wrapped Max and his box carefully inside an old Crush shirt like he was the best present in the whole wide universe. Then I threw my notebook and flashlight that's shaped like a hippopotamus (the light shines from its mouth) into my backpack. Once Ava Claire assured Neely she'd get to bed on time, she gave me a thumbs-up and hung up the phone. Together, we crept downstairs to the kitchen. The hum of the dishwasher, working its magic, masked any sounds we made.

I found the book of matches inside the junk drawer, next to a bottle opener and some random birthday candles. I grabbed the candles on impulse. They were colorful and striped. I liked stripes.

"I'll get Leon," I said to AC. "I don't know what's taking him so long. You collect the snacks."

I darted back up the steps to Leon's room, but he met me on the landing. My jaw dropped. Leon, my impossible brother, had on his best white button-down with the shirttail out, a striped tie he'd obviously tied himself, and a fresh pair of blue jeans. Even his sandy hair looked tamed.

"Ready," he said.

AC let out a squeal of surprise.

I blurted out laughing. "You cannot be serious."

"What?" Leon asked, cheeks red. "Haven't you ever seen a man dressed for a funeral?"

"Your tie's nice," AC said, and glared at me.

"She's right," I said, smoothing my own crumpled tee. "You look . . . improved. Do you have the goods?"

"Out back, under the willow."

I nodded. "Let's do this."

Outdoors, the sun was going to bed, the moon hung low and faint in the sky, and the crickets sang their nightly song. Gravel crunched under our feet as we made our way down the drive to Daddy's shop, really a corner of his boat garage. The shop consisted of the following: a table with a sink, a row of metal cabinets, one swivel stool, a refrigerator/freezer, and an old television that worked sometimes. Daddy said he didn't care a lick about television besides the weather or an occasional game, yet he kept it "for company" while bending wires, threading hooks, or cleaning his day's catch. Thankfully, tonight it worked fine. The Cardinals were playing the Cubs, and Daddy's back was to us.

We crept closer. A motion light kicked on and illuminated a pair of waders left out to dry. We jumped. We'd had so many raccoons and critters over the years, Daddy wouldn't think twice about a tripped security light outside his shop. At least that's what I told myself.

Leon motioned for us to crouch underneath the window.

Following his lead, AC and I slipped along the building into the shadows where our backyard merged with thick brush. The sky turned gray. An owl hooted. I dodged a low branch and brushed cobwebs from my hair. We were close. We reached the willow, and sure enough, behind its weeping limbs sat the sack of sparklers. Just like Leon said. He ran to pick them up while I unzipped my pack and slipped the hippopotamus light's loopy handle around my wrist.

A few more minutes of walking, and Leon announced, "We're here."

I stopped. Ava Claire bumped into me. Even though it was only April, the night was plenty muggy. AC's long hair stuck to the sides of her face. She took a sip from her water bottle, then offered me a drink. I pulled my spare hair tie off my wrist and gave it to her. "It's not pink or sparkly."

"It's perfect. Thanks." She slipped her hair into a low ponytail. "So this is Mud Skull Creek?"

"Yep." I plopped my pack to the ground and began pulling out items. Finding my notebook, I ripped out a page and slipped it into my pocket.

Leon opened the bag of sparklers. "Duct tape?"

"Check."

"Shoebox?"

"What?" I asked.

"In the bottom of your bag. I thought we'd make a boat."

"Okay. Thanks." Wow. Leon was being awfully thoughtful.

I handed him the box and saw he'd already stuffed his socks inside his shoes and had rolled up his blue jeans. I did likewise.

"I hope we don't see any snapping turtles." AC chewed on her fingernail.

"We won't." Leon looked over at her, tearing off another piece of tape. "Are you coming?"

AC shook her head. "I'll watch from here, thanks."

"So this is it." I exhaled and unwound my tee from around Max's box. The shirt fell into a heap on top of my sneakers. I cradled Max in his toothpick box and carried him down the muddy bank. It was dusk now, so the water seemed murkier than usual. Not clean and clear like the water Max was accustomed to. But it wasn't sewer water either. Leon followed me, and I handed him the tiny casket.

He took the birthday candles and taped one in each of the four corners first. I smiled. It was awfully sweet of him (and very un-Leon-like) to not only assist with but dress up for Max's life celebration. He then taped the casket to more cardboard and reached into his back pocket for what I guessed was either the sparklers or Mama's matchbook.

"Wait!" I grabbed his arm.

"What?" He stopped.

"There was something I meant to read first. That's all." I unfolded the page I'd torn out. The sky had grown too dark to see the orange ink, so I clicked on my flashlight, even though I knew the words by heart.

Clearing my throat, I spoke loud enough for Ava Claire to hear me above the creek's babble:

"A Eulogy for Maximus Tropicana, Library Goldfish."

Right away, I was interrupted by the sound of more tape tearing.

"Um. Leon? I'm trying to have a serious moment here."

"Go on. I'm just making sure he's secure."

I cleared my throat and started again:

"Maximus Tropicana was, by all reports, a great library pet. Never once aggressive in his four short years, Max swam in circles, spreading joy to dozens of students occupying Howard County Elementary's library. Max ate his favorite fish flakes at eight every morning. He played hide-and-seek behind the green plant in his fishbowl. Like we didn't know where he really was. Faithful and true, Max lived his aqueous life to the fullest . . . until his scaly gills finally gave out. Many of you know I had the privilege to be Max's charge for the duration of spring break. While we won't know how or why Max was allowed to suffer, please know he handled this adversity with the kind of grace only a true fish holds. The world could use more fish like Max. The end."

"The end," said Ava Claire.

"The end," added Leon, striking a match. The orange ball of flame lit his face, highlighting his long lashes; he really could be all right sometimes, in those rare moments he forgets to pick on me.

"Rest in peace, Max."

The sparklers sputtered to life, spitting flames in the twilight, reflecting in the water. And so, Maximus Tropicana, Beloved Library Fish, began his last swim, down Mud Skull Creek to his final resting place. I stood, my bare feet mud-deep in the cool creek. I wanted to watch him drift away until he snuffed out like a candle in the night.

Only the sky lit up like the flipping Fourth of July. *Screech! Pop. Screech! Pop. Screech! Pop. POP!*

Ava Claire shrieked. I covered my ears and shimmied up the bank. Firecrackers screamed through the air, leaving a glittery wake. "Leon Ulysses Beebe! Those aren't sparklers!"

Leon beamed. "I know! Aren't they GREAT?" *Screech! Screech! Pop.*

"Are you BANANAS?" My voice climbed. "How many did you use?" *Pop! POP!*

"Enough." Leon grinned, all too pleased with his prank. He sprinted up the bank as the last pop pealed through the increasing dark.

I stood shocked, staring into the still of the night. "Goodbye, Max," I whispered.

Pop!

"Come on, Vilonia." AC tugged on my arm. "We've got to get outta here before the neighbors call the cops."

Chapter Seventeen

Iknew as soon as we climbed up the hill back through the brambles that trouble was brewing. Maybe the circling blue and red lights from the patrol car tipped me off. Or the neighbors' frantic footsteps.

I sprinted up to Leon, who had stopped long enough to let a fire engine roar past. "What's going on?" I asked, grabbing his wrist.

"Whatever it is, I don't have a good feeling . . ."

"Hey!" Daddy jogged over to us, carrying a lantern from his shop. "I've been looking for you. The Willoughbys' henhouse is on fire."

"What?" I looked at Leon and then back to my dad. "What about the hens?"

Daddy's lips formed a tight line. "Come on," he said. "We can walk and talk."

I motioned for AC to catch up while Daddy took the lead, his boots crunching gravel underfoot.

"Ransom said he heard bottle rockets go off a few moments before the roof went up in flames. Of course, the hens' bedding is mainly paper and straw . . ."

Leon groaned.

I stopped midtrot, fighting the urge to puke.

"Wait a second." Daddy turned his beam of light to my pack and the empty bag marked SPARKLERS still in Leon's grip. "You two didn't have anything to do with this, did you?"

"Better make that three, Mr. Beebe." Ava Claire.

"We were just trying to give Max a proper burial," I said quietly.

"Max? Who's Max?" Dad ran his fingers through his thick hair.

"Dad, I took the Willoughbys' bag and swapped out their sparklers for old bottle rockets from your shop." Leon kicked some dirt. "But, honest, I didn't know they'd travel so far, especially from down there."

"Down where? The Willoughbys'?"

"No." My stomach churned. "The creek behind their house."

Daddy looked incredulous. "You know . . . just never mind. We can talk later. Mrs. Willoughby is in one heck of a tizzy. You three better start praying these hens are found alive and well." He started in the direction of the smoke.

"Wait!" I called after him. "Were *all* the hens put up for the night?"

117

Daddy shook his head. "Don't know. But Ransom thinks some got out when his mama kicked the door in."

"What about Eleanor?" I asked.

"Eleanor?"

"You know, Eleanor Roostevelt."

"How would I know? They've all got first lady names," Dad replied. "Jackie Kennedy. Martha Washington. Dolley Madison . . . It's like an American history class over there."

I tossed my backpack to Leon as Daddy took off. "The headlamps should be in the front pocket."

"What? Why?" Leon unzipped the bag.

"We're not sitting around like a bunch of bumps on logs. We're going to make things right by finding those hens."

"Okay." Leon shifted into action. "I'll run after Dad while you and AC search by the Nutters'." Leon tossed us each a light.

"Got it." I strapped my lamp to my forehead and helped AC adjust hers.

Turning them on, we followed our bouncing beams of light slicing through the night. Shadowy figures called out, "Martha! Dolley! Mary Todd Lincoln!" But it was too dark to tell which neighbor was which.

Of course, my mind was focused on Eleanor.

"I've never been part of a search and rescue before, much less for a bunch of chickens." AC shined her light up into a tree. "Jackie Kennedy?" she called. "You up there?"

"I only was once, by pure accident . . . Eleanor Roostevelt, where'd you go now?"

The crackle of a walkie-talkie interrupted us. We knew by the clomping sound of boots, plus the walkie-talkie, that it was Deputy Danforth.

"Girls, hang on a minute. We may have a lead . . ."

I turned to face AC, and when I did, the beam of light from my headlamp hit her square in the eyes.

"Ow! Turn your lamp off, you ninny."

"Sorry." I stifled a laugh and looked down.

Deputy Danforth spoke into his receiver. "Go ahead, Eagle."

"Uh, yeah. We have a report of some hens roosting on top of an outbuilding at number twenty-seven Maple Lane."

Ava Claire turned to me, this time shining her light into my eyes. "That's the O'Dells' old horse shed! It backs up to the Willoughbys'."

"Ow." I shielded my eyes. "Great! Let's go."

We cut through the yard, the hens' likely path, and found Mrs. Willoughby dressed in a plaid bathrobe and bunny slippers, her hair in huge curlers, giving Mr. O'Dell an earful. Ransom was halfway up the building on a metal extension ladder, the kind Daddy used to fetch Leon's Frisbees off our roof. Which I guess was exactly what Ransom was doing, only fetching chickens while wearing a hard-hat headlamp.

"You be careful up there, son. We can't have you falling and breaking your neck. The night's already got enough worries."

119

Mr. O'Dell left to move his truck, so its headlights illuminated the hens on the rooftop. Deputy Danforth steered his cruiser around and did the same. That's when Mrs. Willoughby spotted us.

"Oh, girls. What a wild night. First, someone—not my boys, of course, they're far too responsible—goes shooting off bottle rockets well in advance of the festival. Did you hear the girls' horrible screams?" She closed her eyes. Her voice broke. "I'll never be able to forget it as long as I live. Had to bust the door in with a crowbar to let them out. Thank God they all escaped, but now they're scared out of their minds and won't come home. I can't say I blame them." She took a shaky breath. "I got there right as the roof caved in."

"Holy Chihuahuas," I whispered.

Mrs. Willoughby wiped away a tear. "Yes, sweet Dolley is in shock. A fireman found her running headlong into trees and shrubs."

"I'm so sorry," I whispered, at a loss for what else to say.

"She'll survive. My priority now is to get the rest of the brood to safety before a predator eats them for dinner."

Mrs. Willoughby took a sip of coffee from a Thermos, never taking her eyes off Ransom and his brother Rory, who held the ladder steady. Ransom took his first step onto the roof and slid a few inches. Mrs. Willoughby drew a sharp breath. "Nice of you gals to come out and help. Especially with the festival tomorrow."

"We want to help," I said. I didn't mention it was 100 percent our fault her hens were homeless. "Any sign of Eleanor?"

"Not yet, but it's hard to see in the dark. We've counted seven birds in all. So that'd be all of them, but it's hard to say if we've counted anyone twice. The boys will have to catch them one at a time and hand them down." In the glow of my headlamp, I saw her eyes water.

"I'll catch her, don't you worry." The words flew out of my mouth before I could stop them.

Mrs. Willoughby really looked at me for the first time since we'd walked up. "That's mighty kind of you, Vi. But there's no way I'll let you on top of that shed in the dark. Your daddy would never fry fish for me again. Maybe you and AC could hold the ladder so that Rory could climb on up."

"Sure." I shrugged and walked over as Ransom inched his way across the roof toward Jackie Kennedy.

"Hey, Rory."

"Hey," he replied, keeping his eyes on his brother's progress.

"Your mama said I could hold the ladder if you want to help Ransom. He'll need someone at the top to hand the hens to, won't he?"

"I guess. If he can catch one."

"He's a Willoughby. Catching chickens is in your DNA."

Rory looked at me and smiled. I repeat, Rory Willoughby smiled.

At me.

Good thing it was dark, as my face turned redder than an heirloom tomato. I tried to look like I was telepathically helping Ransom nab Jackie. By the cheers, I could tell he'd gotten her too. Those Willoughbys were stealth.

"Well? Aren't ya going up?" I asked.

It was Rory's turn to blush. "I'm not a fan of heights, to be honest."

"What?"

"You heard me."

My mouth dropped. "Well, you hold the ladder steady, 'cause I'm climbing."

I adjusted my headlamp and gripped the first rung, then the next. The metal creaked beneath me. Don't look down. Don't. Look.

I looked.

Lights and people and Howard County's news crew swirled under my feet. "They called the *news*?" Sweet pugs. I shut my eyes and counted to twenty, because ten wasn't high enough for this nonsense.

"You're almost there, Vilonia. Two more steps." Rory might be a prankster, but he could be your biggest cheerleader, too.

I hoisted myself as high as the roof.

"Welcome to the party." Ransom met me at the top, holding a rattled hen.

"How many more are there?" I asked, stretching my hand out for Jackie.

"Six. You okay to carry her down?"

"I carried myself up here, didn't I?"

"Yeah you did, but I need your help catching them." He turned his head and motioned to Dawson, the O'Dell boy who'd been an extra in too many films to list. "Dawson, think you can carry this bird down?"

Dawson nodded, pulled a comb from his back pocket, and ran it through his hair.

Oh brother.

I stepped onto the roof, and Dawson disappeared down the ladder with Jackie.

Ransom rolled his eyes. "Some people aren't cut out for hen management. Okay. Here's what you need to know. Chickens are virtually blind at night, but you've got to move quiet and slow. You can't startle them. Keep your light dim and pointed down, like this."

"Got it."

"Grab them gently over their wings and hold them close, like you're protecting a—"

"Football."

"Or baby." He laughed. "You've got this."

And that's how I ended up on top of the O'Dells' horse barn well past my bedtime, catching chickens. We nabbed them one by one and passed them down the ladder to waiting volunteers. First there was Martha Washington, then Mary Todd Lincoln, Frances Cleveland, Rosalynn Carter, and Harriet Lane.

"Harriet Lane? Don't you mean Lois Lane?" I asked.

Ransom snorted. "Lois Lane was first lady only to Superman. *Harriet* Lane acted as first lady for her uncle, President James Buchanan. He never married."

Seeing how Ransom talked sweet and low to his runaway hens, I predicted he'd never have that issue if he was elected president.

He wiped sweat from his brow and grinned at me all sheepish. "We got one more to catch. And she's a runner."

"Eleanor Roostevelt," I guessed, and scanned the rooftop. "Where is she now?"

"That way." He pointed to the far side. "She's ruffled and awake."

"Perfect," I said. "So am I."

Chapter Eighteen

Remembering Ransom's advice, I crept along the roof like a ninja assassin.

"Hey, Ellie," I whispered as I stole close. She flapped her wings and clucked a string of curses. "Simmer down. I know your universe has imploded, but that's no way to speak to someone—especially someone trying to save your tail. And I'm sorry, but the great outdoors is not the safest place for a hen to spend the night." I stretched out my hand. Another flurry of wings and feathers cut the night. I turned to Ransom. He shrugged. Eleanor wasn't going without a fight.

Think, Vilonia. You earned her trust once.

"Ransom! Throw me your shirt."

"What? No."

"Trust me." I held out my hand.

He looked at me like I'd lost my mind. "There are cameras down there."

"Come on. Do it." I waved my fingers to signal I was

waiting. "Your mama will never forgive you if you leave her best laying hen behind."

He huffed but peeled off his shirt and threw it my way. The soft fabric smelled of sweaty socks and fresh-cut grass. I nodded thanks and inched forward, my legs getting the shakes. Eleanor, however, stared straight ahead. Maybe she was night-blind. In one swift move, I wrapped her wings in Ransom's shirt like I had with my softball towel the week before.

And when she laid her feathery head against my chest as we made our way down the ladder to cheers and flashing cameras, I'd like to think she forgave me for burning her coop to the ground.

Once the hens were put in the garage for the night and the fire truck had rolled away, Leon, AC, and I told Deputy Danforth the honest truth of how Max's memorial skyrocketed from glowing to explosive.

After a few questions, he flipped his notebook shut. "That should do it," he said. "Why don't you kids hop in, and I'll give you a lift home."

None of us had ridden in a cop car before, but we were too tired to appreciate the excitement.

Daddy met us out front with ice-cold glasses of water. His beard looked grayer, and his eyes wore tired like one of Mama's faded sweatshirts. Maybe the light from the stars played tricks, but I bet not.

We hopped out, and he and the deputy exchanged a few words.

After the cruiser pulled away, Daddy said, "I don't know how or where to begin." A vein in his forehead pulsed. "You guys got lucky. Someone could have been hurt, bad."

"Yes, sir," I said, taking my drink. The others nodded. We were too thirsty, tuckered, and plumb terrified to speak.

"Deputy Danforth just filled me in about the fish. A fish!" He sighed like he couldn't believe a tiny goldfish could cause such calamity.

"Sorry, Daddy," I whispered. Sweat ran down my back, and I took another sip.

For the first time all evening, I noticed the full moon overhead. It looked distant and small, like an approaching train at the far end of a dark tunnel. A ring of light encircled it.

"Moon halo," Daddy said. "Rain's coming."

The screen door creaked and a voice called, "Hello?"

I could barely make out Mama standing under our flickering porch light. One of Nana's quilts engulfed her. "Are the kids all right? I've made toast."

My stomach perked up at that magic word, and I licked my lips. One thing Nana had taught Mama that Mama taught me was to never underestimate the comforting powers of perfectly toasted toast.

"They're fine, Janet. We'll be right in."

The door banged shut, and Daddy pinched the bridge

of his nose and sighed again. "We'll talk about the fine mess you've made in the morning, once I've calmed down and everyone's rested. Now grab some toast, brush your teeth, and hop to bed."

While my parents discussed our fate on the front porch, we did as we were told. Leon must have felt rotten for firing the rockets in the first place, because he skipped toast altogether, went straight to his room, and locked his door.

Ava Claire took her toast and nicely folded pajamas down the hall to the bathroom. "I'd better bathe first. Neely's going to be so mad if she hears I'm still awake and filthy."

I sunk onto my bed, nibbling my toast, not caring whether I brushed my teeth tonight or not. I was exhausted and my heart felt like a wrung-out sponge.

I wasn't prepared for how tired and angry Daddy would be. Usually he could keep his cool in front of AC, but tonight he had fallen apart like shattered glass. The Willoughbys' chicken coop was now a smoldering pile of debris and would need to be completely rebuilt. And that cost money we couldn't spare. And Dolley. Poor Dolley, I hoped Mrs. Willoughby was right that she'd recover.

I tugged off my muddy jeans and slipped into my pajamas. Only when I was tossing my clothes into the hamper did I remember the adoption flyer.

Ray Charles.

I bit my lip. Did I even deserve him after all the damage

I'd caused? I took another bite of toast—thick, buttery sour-dough, doused in cinnamon and brown sugar. Maybe I no longer deserved Ray Charles, but my mama did. She deserved to get better. We needed her to get better.

And Ray Charles needed a forever home. Shoot, we all needed each other.

The paper crinkled as I smoothed its creases. I studied the phone number, a local one. It clearly stated to call if interested, but the alarm clock on my nightstand said 9:47 p.m. Did I dare call? I hadn't filled out a proper adoption application, because, well, my parents were against it. And with my luck, the people who'd ripped off the other numbers were in line ahead of me. But this was Ray Charles. At least, I think it was. Would the person who answered the phone even take the time to talk to a kid?

There was one way to find out. As Nana always said, "Here goes something."

Grabbing the phone, I crept down the stairs and into the laundry room, pulling the door shut behind me. The dryer rocked back and forth, tossing a load of towels. The mechanical whine provided the right amount of humming to mask my voice, good since my parents were still up. I hopped on top of the machine and took a deep breath. My fingers shook as I dialed each number. Pressing the phone to my ear, I waited for the ring. My heels kicked the front of the machine. Thud, thud, thud. A ring.

I hung up.

"Chicken," I said to myself. "Okay, this time's for real."

I dialed again. I closed my eyes, waiting. It rang. Once. Twice. I wiped my sweaty palms on my pajamas.

"Hello?" a lady answered. She sounded youngish. A television blared in the background.

"Uh. Hi," I said. *Don't be a dork. Don't be a dork.* "I'm calling about the flyer at Pete's Pets? For the dog?"

"Yes," she said. The background noise stopped. "About Izzy? What would you like to know?"

"Well, is he still available?" I asked, pretty sure I sounded exactly like a dork.

"Yes. But he's not quite ready for a new home."

"Oh?" Something in the back of my mind told me I knew this voice.

"Still needs his shots, *and* his mama rejected him, so he's bottle fed." She gave a big sigh, like this last bit of information annoyed her and kept her from painting her nails or finishing her favorite show. Or maybe she was put out that the mama rejected her own pup. "But he's a sweetheart. He even has a heart-shaped button nose."

Ray Charles! I knew it.

"Right." I tried to not get my hopes up. "How would I go about adopting him?"

"Well"—her voice took on a friendly tone—"for starters, you'd need to come in and meet him and fill out an application either in person or online, if you haven't already. And at least one adult member of the family must visit him too. Preferably, we'd like to see how he gets along with the entire family, but someone over the age of eighteen must be present."

"Okay," I said, like that was no big deal. "What if my parents work?"

"We have weekend hours. And I'll have a booth with a few of our dogs at the Catfish Festival."

The Festival! My heart picked up.

"Will Izzy be there?" I scrunched my face up at the name they'd given him. Ray Charles was so *not* an Izzy.

"Hmm. It will depend on how he's doing that day, and if anyone else adopts him between now and then. But probably not."

"Oh." My voice deflated. "So you've had other calls."

"A few. And some forms in the queue. But Izzy's small, and it's our job to match him with the best home."

"Yeah. I was hoping that'd be ours. My parents are working the festival, and I know once they saw him, they'd see his potential."

The lady didn't say anything for a moment. "Maybe he can visit for a few moments, later in the evening."

"Oh, that'd be great!" I tried not to squeal. It was hard.

"I'm not making any promises, though."

"Gotcha. And what website has the application form?"

"The Howard County Animal Shelter dot org."

"Got it. Thanks!" I said, a little too chipper.

"No problem," the lady said. "What did you say your name was?"

My name! "Oh. My friends call me Vi."

"Well, Vi. Do you have any other questions?"

"Probably, but it's past my bedtime. Kids my age need ten to eleven hours of sleep a night for optimal health and growth."

"Well, thanks for calling. Buh-bye."

Click.

Buh-bye? Hadn't I heard that somewhere before?

"Good-bye," I replied, even though she'd already disconnected. "And by the way, the best home is ours." I slid off the dryer and marched upstairs to bed, happy and full of hope. If I couldn't bring Ray Charles home to Mama and Daddy, then maybe I could bring them to Ray Charles. I now had two missions to complete at the Catfish Festival. 1) Win a goldfish. 2) Adopt a dog.

Chapter Nineteen

The smell of bacon frying woke me. I rubbed sleep from my eyes, and the early Saturday sun peeked through my window. It looked to be a beautiful day for a festival.

Ava Claire snoozed next to me, wearing her scratchy-looking pink pajamas and a frilly satin sleeping mask. She said the mask blocked out any trace of light and was infused with aromatic lavender oil to reduce stress and encourage relaxation. I told her that's what curtains and ice cream were for. I sat up, slowly, to keep from creaking the bed (and disrupting her beauty sleep) and slipped out from under the covers. Ava Claire didn't even roll over when I tripped over a pillow and bumped my knee. Maybe she slept in therapeutic earplugs as well.

"Good morning, Frog," Daddy said, and plopped a steaming waffle onto a plate. "Feel like waffles today?"

My stomach rumbled, fully awakened. "I feel like waffles every day." And that was the honest truth. I scooted to the table, gloriously unaware of my horrendous display of bed-head.

"Bacon?"

"Please."

"One piece or two?"

I gave him a look.

He put three on my plate. "Where's Toad?"

"Sleeping." I poured myself a glass of orange juice from the carton on the table. "Where's Leon?"

"Running."

I took a sip of juice.

"And Mama?" I asked, already guessing the answer.

"She's having a bit of trouble getting going after all of the commotion late last night. And the headline this morning." He slapped the *Howard County Press* down next to my plate.

COOP CATCHES FIRE AFTER FIREWORK PRANK screamed the headline in big black letters. A giant photograph of the smoldering henhouse followed by a full-length article highlighting the damage covered most of the page. A quote from Mrs. Willoughby was enlarged and bolded, but I didn't even read it. The tiny byline and profile picture of the journalist told me plenty. Bettina B. Wiggins. *Poodles.*

"It wasn't a true prank." I turned the paper over. A picture of Dawson O'Dell cradling a terrified hen in his arms glared at me. *Jackie.* I groaned and put my head down, unable to look at the article any longer. "I'm sorry, Daddy."

"Yeah. Me too." Daddy plunked two plates sided with

thick strips of bacon on the table, one across from the other. Warmth from the waffle radiated onto my face. Five minutes before, I'd have licked my lips in anticipation, but now I didn't think I could eat five bites. "The whole world knows, but no one knows the truth." I dredged a strip of bacon through my maple syrup. "We weren't being malicious . . ."

"The people that matter know. However, you three need to apologize to Mrs. Willoughby in person." Daddy took a bite of waffle, then blotted his mouth with his napkin.

I nodded and poked at my waffle.

"And." Daddy's face brightened. "You'll be able to tonight, as you are now working alongside me in the Tom Sawyer food truck."

My fork clattered to my plate. "WHAT?"

"Simmer down." Daddy held up his palms. "It's only fair you guys work a few hours to pay for the damage."

"But, we'll miss the festival!" I jumped up, knocking my chair backward.

"No, you'll technically still be there. And if AC agrees to work one hour, then you only have to work two."

"But this is all Leon's fault! He's the one who shot the fireworks, not me. Not her!" My voice squeaked with frustration.

"And he'll work longer than you, but you were all present. You know better than to sneak down to the creek at night without permission."

Speechless, I snatched a piece of bacon from my plate and

bit off the syrupy end. My head spun. How could I win Mr. Reyes a new goldfish and introduce Mama and Daddy to Ray Charles if I was scooping up mounds of coleslaw? And what about AC? She was dancing a number in the pageant!

"Vilonia?" Daddy asked as I carried my dishes to the sink. "Aren't you going to finish your breakfast? We Beebes don't pass up fresh-squeezed orange juice."

"Sorry, Daddy," I said, scraping waffle bits into the trash. "Guess I'm not feeling very Beebe-ish today. Gotta run."

So I ran. Ran right out the door. Because only one thing made me feel better when I was down in the dumps or beyond frustrated. Okay, two things. A Guy's Cookie Dough Blast was most definitely up there, but I needed something physical. Ava Claire danced. Leon ran. Me?

I pitched.

And pitched. And pitched. I pitched so much I became a quick pick for games at recess. And on a good day, when I wore my lucky socks, I could throw a curve so fine it made boys weep. I didn't have my lucky socks today, they were in the wash, but I did have my glove and my wire basket full to the brim with worn softballs. So I lugged them out to the best spot in the yard, by the tire swing.

Dropping the basket and glove in the grass, I walked up to the old tire, grabbed it through its middle, and pulled it back a few steps. A fly buzzed my face. I blew my bangs out of my eyes with a puff and counted, "One, two, *three*!" Then I took off running and heaved that dusty tire with everything in me so it sailed up into the air and cleared its branch. When it came down on the other side, its rope had shortened, lifting the tire a couple of inches off the ground to create a strike zone. One more swing around the branch did the trick. I stopped the tire's pendulum swing and stepped back to survey its height. Golden. Plucking the first ball from the basket, I warmed my arm. My foot dug its place in the earth. My fingers gripped the skin of the ball, while my glove and eye found my target. I stood like a deer in the woods, all senses alert. My heart thumped. My nostrils flared. *This is for you, Ray Charles.*

In a flash, my left arm swung back and around. The ball flew from my grasp. It sliced through the air and straight through the tire's middle.

"Yes! Take that, world!" I danced a jig. Over and over, I threw one ball after another—for Max, for Mama, for Ray Charles, for *me*. All my anger and sadness and frustration soared through the air with each pitch. Soon, I'd finished the basket.

When AC found me, I was picking up the last ball. It had sailed clear to the back fence.

"Hey!" She tromped through the grass toward me, wearing my horse head T-shirt, the only shirt I owned with a speck of glitter. "Heard you skipped breakfast."

I waved my glove. "Yeah. Guess you heard we're working the Willoughbys' food truck."

"Yeah." She wrinkled her nose. "Sorry. I don't do fish."

"I know. Fish eyes. Fish scales. Fish tails. Fish smells . . ." I tossed the last ball into the air and caught it.

Ava Claire shuddered. "Yeah. I meant, I don't think I can work."

"Excuse me?" I tossed the ball into the basket. "We are working to pay for the chicken coop."

"I know, but Neely said maybe I could come up with something not fish related, like manis and pedis for a cause or something."

My jaw dropped. "Are you skipping out on me?"

"What? No!" Her cheeks burned. "It's just I can't miss the pageant. My dance teacher's competing, and remember, I'm dancing in the second number."

"But"—I threw my glove into the basket for good measure—"you can't walk away and leave me!"

"You can't expect me to smell like fish. It's my first solo!"

Great. Just great. Ava Claire adored her dance teacher Miss Connelly, and if anyone could recite the past decade of Miss Catfish tiara wearers, it was my best friend. She dreamed of two, no three, things: 1) completing a quadruple pirouette 2) one day being crowned Miss Catfish, and 3) one day being crowned Miss Catfish without having to actually sample said catfish. This was a perfect stepping-stone, a big deal, and I was sunk.

"Aren't you happy for me?" she asked.

"No! I mean, yes. Of course I am, but your timing is

plain crummy. A real friend would help."

AC frowned. "A real friend would be more supportive of my first solo performance."

"You're one to talk, Miss I Have Dance Every Day. You've hardly been around, and I'm trying to replace someone's pet and adopt a dog while working a food truck."

"Maybe so, but you're not the only one with stuff going on," AC said, and crossed her arms. "And I have too been here. I helped with Max. I went to his memorial at the creek, and you know how I feel about snakes. I even hunted hens in the dark."

"Okay, fine. You're right. Maybe I haven't been the best friend. But things have been a bit nuts around here, in case you haven't noticed!"

"You don't have to shout."

"Okay, okay. I'm sorry." I sighed. "But I still need to win a goldfish to be responsible, and somehow, someway get my parents to meet Ray Charles at the Animal Shelter booth. *If* he's even there." My voice became a whine. "If we both work, my time will be cut. You have to help me, AC. The Great Pet Campaign is on the line."

She looked skeptical. "You know fish makes me faint."

"*Please.* You'll be done in plenty of time to get backstage, and I'll have enough time to find a goldfish and watch you perform. It's win-win."

AC tightened her braid and sighed.

I practiced some deep breaths.

"Fine," she huffed. "I'll work one hour, max. Only because it's Ray Charles. He'd better be as cute as you say he is."

"Thank you!" I surprised her with a big hug. "I knew I could count on you."

"But if I miss my call time . . ."

"Do you really think I'd do that to you?"

She raised her eyebrows.

"Yeah, okay." I crossed my arms. "Have a little faith."

AC looked at me. "I'm warning you, though, if the announcer takes the stage and I'm still working, I can't promise a buttermilk biscuit or cup of sweet tea won't go AWOL along with me."

"A-what?"

"A-*wall*. A. W. O. L. Absent without official leave. It's a military term."

"Oh." I glanced at the silver locket the general had given her before he left, the locket full of memories and meaning and missing. "Sorry. I didn't know. Have you heard anything?"

AC shook her head. "But it's okay. Neely thinks we'll hear from him soon. Anyway, I need to get ready for dress rehearsal, so I'll catch you later. You're welcome to ride with us. Maybe we could squeeze in a few rides before the gate opens and we have to clock in?" She smiled.

"Sure," I said, picking up the basket of balls. "Maybe that'll be just enough time to win myself a goldfish."

Chapter Twenty

ow that Ava Claire had left, I had a chunk of time before the festival to work on any new obits from the day before. Luckily, the laptop was still in the dining room where Mama had left it. Even better, Mama was holed up in her bedroom devouring cooking shows. Thank you, Food Channel's Cupcake Week. Still, Leon and Daddy could finish making lures in the shop at any moment. I had to act fast.

Opening Mama's e-mail, I saw straightaway one had come through in the middle of the night. It had a little red exclamation mark, marking it urgent. The sender was bettina@howardcountypress.com. I suppressed an eye roll. Miss Bettina probably called a supermarket ad for foot cream urgent. I clicked anyway.

The subject line read *Bob Lafferty, ASAP*.

Who on earth was Bob Lafferty? I read on:

Dear Janet,

I need the Lafferty obit by 2:00 p.m. today. I dropped it by your house in a manila envelope. Vilonia said she'd make sure you saw it. You have, haven't you? I know he's not from here, but his VIP family is, and they wanted his obit run yesterday. I need this today, or I'll be forced to find someone else to write it, or heaven forbid, write the thing myself.

Call me.

—BW

Good gravy on a biscuit! The time on Mama's laptop read ten till noon. That gave me two hours to turn this obit around. I leaned back in my seat and thought hard. The envelope Miss Bettina gave me before we noticed Max was sick . . . where was it?

I circled the living room for the manila envelope. I looked under the sofa, the tables. I even lifted the rug. It wasn't behind the couch cushions. Nor was it left on top of the piano or placed inside the bench. Mama must have moved it. But where?

If I remembered correctly, *Janet* was scrawled in red. So no one should have touched it but Mama. Or me, but I hadn't. Obviously.

I trudged back to the dining room, where the laptop sat on Nana's old honey oak table. In the center sat a huge bowl full of dusty wooden Easter eggs. Mama was never any good at switching out the holiday stuff. I turned to the wicker basket on the buffet, jammed full with bills, catalogs, and miscellaneous mailers forwarded from Nana's address. It was too painful for Mama look through them. Daddy and I should have a mail opening party one night. We'd watch the Weather Channel and sip frosty root beers.

I thumbed through the envelopes on the top and tossed aside a flyer for lawn care because that was what Leon was for, thank you very much. And another for laundry service because, well, that was my job now. Forget it, Mama hadn't touched this basket in weeks. The mailer wasn't here, and I was wasting precious time.

I spun around to check her bedroom, when something crinkled under my foot. I lifted my shoe. It was a Little Debbie wrapper. I ran to the wastebasket. Two more. My heart jumped. Someone had bought Little Debbies. And hadn't Mama found her car keys in the pantry once, between the pasta and the potato chips? I zipped to the kitchen and swung the pantry door wide.

The stepstool squeaked across the floor. I hopped up, skipping right over cans of beans and stewed tomatoes, even ignoring the jars of peanut butter and marshmallow crème, to shove aside Mama's canisters of sugar, flour, nuts, baking chips, and Dutch cocoa powder. Then, voilà! Two boxes of snack cakes appeared in the way back—*and* resting on top of them was just the envelope I needed. An 8.5x11 manila one labeled *Janet* in red ink, last seen three days ago in the living room.

Shoving the envelope under my arm, I marched back to the dining room with a jar of marshmallow crème, a spoon, and one looming deadline. While the first spoonful of fluff melted on my tongue, I tore open the envelope, revealing its contents. The first item, a sticky note, read:

Dr. Robert Lafferty, age 70, of Springdale, AR, died Thursday, April 16.

Something whirred in my brain. I knew that name. I turned it over in my mind, scrutinizing it from all sides. Robert Lafferty . . . Bob Lafferty? There was a Dr. Bob Lafferty mentioned in the baby book Mama had made to record all my important firsts—first slept through the night, first step, first tooth, first food, first word, first doctor visit. Whoa, did that mean . . . ?

I scanned the pages of photographs and newspaper clippings.

Yes.

My heart whispered the obvious truth. Dr. Robert Lafferty was the one Nana had sung praises of every year since my birth. The emergency room doctor who'd massaged my chest with his flat thumbs, willing my feeble heart to kick-start. *Lub-dub, lub-dub.*

The doctor for whom my grateful mama had baked a separate from-scratch cake celebrating my first birthday and every one after that, until he retired and moved away before I was four. Mama said you never could repay goodness like that.

Before I came home, all she knew to do while days stretched into weeks, and weeks into months, was to tie an apron around her waist and bake. *Lots of prayers are lifted while flour's sifted,* Nana would say with a wink.

So here I was, snacking on marshmallow fluff, sitting criss-cross applesauce in a dining room chair, and typing up my doctor's obit:

Dr. Robert "Bob" Lafferty, age 70, of Springdale, AR, slid into home on Thursday, April 16. Born October 22, 1944, to hardworking dairy farmers, Lafferty's childhood revolved around two things: baseball and milking the family's cows. A stickler for being on time, Lafferty was a teacher's dream. He was tardy once—the day his cows, Pearl and Spalding, escaped the fence and created a grand slam of a traffic jam. Always keeping his eye on the ball, Lafferty shocked no one when he was accepted to medical school at the University of Mississippi ('70). He practiced family medicine at Mercy Hospital and had the honor of catching countless newborns—singles, doubles, even a couple of triples. Left to cherish Dr. Lafferty's stats are his mother; his sister, Olivia (Brooks) of

Power Alley, MS; his faithful dog and companion, Deuce; and a host of extended family, friends, and hospital staff. A celebration of Bob's life will take place at 2:00 p.m., Friday, at Christ the King Cathedral, Springdale, AR. Don't be late or you're out! To make it a double-header, a smaller, separate memorial will follow in Howard County, MS, in Mercy Hospital's Chapel. This date is to be determined. In lieu of flowers, donations may be made to the Northwest Arkansas Animal Shelter or Marchofdimes.org. Play ball!

With the press of a button, I launched the obit through cyberspace to Miss Bettina's computer, and the cycle of life smacked me square on the head. "Thank *you*, Dr. Lafferty," I whispered to the air around me. "Thank you for not quitting on me." My mind drifted to the pet store photograph of Izzy, aka Ray Charles, whose stare seemed to say, *And thank* you *for not quitting on me.*

My heart fluttered *lub-dub, lub-dub* for maybe the gazillionth time in my life, and I thought of Daddy, and all the worrying he did then and now, and of Mama, and her Infinite Sadness hanging low like a cloud, and suddenly I knew there was no way, no how, I'd quit on Ray Charles. Not without a fight. Because that's what I'd always been, a fighter. Nana said.

I bowed my head right then and there, even though it wasn't anywhere near mealtime. Nana said the good Lord wasn't bound by time. He'd listen anytime, anywhere, if your heart needed to speak. I squeezed my eyes tight, folded my hands, and prayed.

Dear Lord, it's me, Vilonia Beebe. I live in the tire swing house on Walleye Street, but I guess you know that. I wanted to talk about, well, lots of things. For starters, I'd appreciate it if Ray Charles got matched to a good home, preferably ours. He can't go somewhere where they'll name him Izzy. You know better than anyone he's not Izzy material. I just know he'd do Mama's heart good, like a big dose of nasty-tasting cherry-flavored medicine that you want to spit out, but in the end, you force it down like a brave soldier. And hallelujah, it does make everything better, like it promises right there on the bottle. I guess what I mean is Ray Charles could bring back Mama's laugh. Is that in the Holy Bible somewhere? About laughter working like cherry-flavored medicine? And what makes a person more happy than cuddling a puppy? . . . Okay, maybe cuddling a baby hedgehog. But it's against state law to domesticate one—I know because Leon looked it up on the Internet once. And God, you know Leon's trying out for track team. And I still need a goldfish. That's a long story. . . . And I know you see Daddy working to keep our house one step under chaos (his words, not mine) and, well, sometimes he washes my clothes on the hot cycle, and they shrink up two sizes too small. That leaves me wearing Leon's old baseball jersey that says ROACH CARPET & TYLE *in ironed-on letters. Speaking of dads, AC's dad is still deployed. So keep an eye on him, too, would you? And one more thing. Please tell Nana I've grown a quarter of an inch. Over and out.*

    Amen.

Chapter Twenty-One

The screen door banged, and I about jumped out of my skin.

"Vi?" Daddy called. "Leon and I are headed to the fairgrounds, if you want to hitch a ride."

"No thanks, I'm going with AC in a bit."

"All right, be sure to check in. And take your raincoat. There's a chance."

I looked outside.

"Vi? Did you hear me? Take your raincoat."

"But . . ."

"The weather is a great bluffer. E. B.—"

"E. B. White, Daddy. I know."

The door slammed into place behind him. I opened the dining window a smidgen and watched his truck rumble away. A spring breeze rustled the grass while a yellow butterfly danced across blade tips. There wasn't a cloud in the sky. Daddy's barometer was hardly ever wrong, but outside didn't smell like rain, not one bit. I shut the window with a sigh.

It was a perfect day, pretty as a painting. And I got to spend it stuck inside a food truck.

I swiped dust from the computer screen with my elbow and opened Mama's browser. A quick search took me straight to the Animal Shelter's home page. One click later, I stared at their official adoption form and thirty detailed questions.

What is your primary reason for adopting a dog?
Describe your home. Do you rent or own? Do you have a fence?
Who will be the primary caregiver of the dog?
Do you travel?
How many hours per day will the dog be left alone?
Do you presently have a dog or any other pets?
Has a member of your family experienced animal-related allergies?
Where will the dog sleep?
Do you feel obedience training makes a dog a better companion?

"Schnoodles. And I thought Mrs. Crewel's math tests were long." I scrolled to the bottom of the questionnaire: *You must be eighteen or older to sign this form.* Ugh. I put my head down on the table and moaned. I'm *half* of eighteen. That math I could do.

"Forget it." I exited the website and left Mama's laptop

exactly as I'd found it. But I still had half an hour to kill before AC arrived, so I wandered outside to the tree house.

Other than my bedroom, it was my favorite place to think.

I climbed up the rope ladder, past the NO TRESPASSING sign Leon had nailed to the trunk years ago. He'd all but stopped coming, saying he was too busy, but I knew what he meant was too old. Whatever. Even Nana had climbed up here once for tea and cookies. If I ever got too old or cool for tree houses, it'd be a sad day.

The trapdoor swung open with a little shove. I stuck my head through the opening and squinted at the light that spilled through the window. Hauling myself up, I shut the door behind me, safety first, and then turned around to survey the space. Everything was in its proper place, from the pair of beanbags slumped in the corner like gossiping friends to the tub of well-read books beside them. Drawings and photographs pinned to the far wall fluttered whenever the wind blew through. And the shelf of Mason jars holding essentials like jellybeans, trail mix, and Twizzlers brightened up the wooden space. I smiled. It really was a magical place, especially when the twinkle lights worked. Ray Charles would love it up here. I could already envision a jar for doggie treats.

I grabbed a twist of licorice and walked over to the photo wall.

There was a picture of Mama and Daddy sitting in Daddy's boat out on the lake. The sun shone in the background, and Mama, with her polished toes propped on the side, laughed under a big floppy hat.

That's the Mama I miss. I tugged on the Twizzler with my teeth. Another photo, a faded one, in a plain black frame made me pause. *Nana.* I swallowed.

Nana's face was smooth, not wrinkled, and she looked thinner than I ever remembered seeing her. Still, something lurked behind her round glasses that I recognized. Fire.

No, resolve.

Maybe I was a bit like her. I took another bite.

Rap, tap, rappity-tap. AC's secret knock echoed through the fort.

I lifted the door.

"Ready to work the festival?" She poked her head through.

"Sure." I smiled. "Let me tell Mama."

I walked through the house, but Mama was nowhere to be found. Her bed was made for the first time since I don't know when. The TV was off. The kitchen sat clean and empty. I poked my head into the dining room and saw straightaway that while the pile of mail was still there, her computer was gone. She couldn't have gone far. Her minivan still sat in the garage. Then a sound like angels' wings drifted inside, and I knew where Mama was. The screened porch.

I slid the door open and stepped into a mini oasis. Thanks to Daddy and I, most of the plants had survived. I'm sure they missed Mama's daily watering and talking to. And Nana's plants probably missed her singing. She had hung Nana's wind chimes, made from multicolored beads, a silver teapot, and half a dozen hodgepodge teaspoons. I closed my eyes and listened to the jingling. It was almost like Nana was on the porch swing beside me, patting my hand and sipping peach tea.

"Mama?" I whispered. She tried to hide behind her computer, but I'd already seen the river of tears rolling down her cheeks. "Are you all right?"

Mama dabbed her eyes with a tissue and closed her laptop. "Yeah, baby. I'm going through some old e-mails."

My heart stopped. "Oh. What kind of e-mails?" *Don't say "work," please don't say "work."*

"Oh, you know. People. Friends. Coworkers . . . Nana." Mama sniffled. "She made the worst typos. But enough of that. What do you need?"

"I'm headed to the festival a little early with Ava Claire. We wanted to check out some rides before working the truck." I wound the bottom of my T-shirt around my finger, waiting for my old mama's "absolutely not without an adult" and the following lecture on the dangers of street carnivals.

But she simply said, "Sure. Go ahead. Stick together and don't spend all your money on cotton candy. It's bad for your teeth."

I lit up like a firefly. "Yes, ma'am. Thank you, Mama!" I hugged her neck, skipped back to the sliding door, and paused. I couldn't leave her like this. Turning around, I asked, "You think you'll come? It's so nice out. But if you ask Daddy what he thinks, the weather's always—"

"Bluffing," we said in unison.

Mama smiled for a moment and then laughed a laugh softer than the tinkling wind chimes. I laughed too, surprised. I'd waited two months to hear that sound.

"Listen up, you," Mama said, drying her eyes. "Let's meet by the Ferris wheel when the fireworks start. Now skedaddle. I've got some calls to make." And she shooed me away with her crinkled tissue.

I didn't ask twice, I just gave her a confused are-you-sure look. She threw a Mama-knows-best look right back. And my heart flopped like a catfish on dry land. Mama hadn't given me one of those looks since . . . well, Before.

I hurried up to my room and grabbed ten bucks from the jelly jar in my closet. I'd just shoved the bill in my back pocket, when what did I spy? My raincoat. I picked it up off the floor. It had big pockets, which would be useful if I won a few things, or one main thing. Like a goldfish. So I tied it around my middle, even though I'd roast like a turkey at Thanksgiving, and flew down the stairs to meet AC.

"Hey, slowpoke. What took so long?"

"Oh, nothing. Just Mama."

"Why'd you bring your raincoat?"

"Daddy."

AC laughed and grabbed my wrist. "Come on. Let's ride some rides!"

Chapter Twenty-Two

Jazz music filled the streets as we neared the fairgrounds. A huge banner announcing *Howard County's 47th Annual CATFISH FESTIVAL* stretched above the entrance, and beyond that was a kaleidoscope of colors, sights, and sounds. My skin tingled with excitement.

The line to get in snaked quickly through roped-off lanes to the ticket booth. We paid five dollars for the twelve-and-under all-you-can-ride wristband and took off. Giddy, AC dug her fingernails into my wrist. We flew past the little kids' area of inflatables and bouncy houses to the Mirror Maze. No line. *Yeah!* We giggled and showed the worker our bands, and she waved us in.

"Now what?" I asked, stumbling back out into the daylight. "We have time for one more ride."

AC frowned. She still wasn't down with working. But a promise was a promise. Loud music boomed from a gigantic speaker next to us, and we jumped. AC screamed over the blast, "Look, Vi! The Himalaya!"

She zipped off, and I followed her bobbing ballerina bun through the crowd. We rode frontward, then backward, then frontward again. *Bumpity-bump. Bump.* With loud, awful music blaring the whole time. Nana would so not have approved.

"What about the Ferris wheel?" AC asked, out of breath from so much squealing.

I thought for a moment, thinking of what Mama had said about meeting up. "We should save that for later, when we can see porch lights for miles. Anyway, we'd better check in with Daddy."

AC wrinkled her nose. "Yeah. I guess so."

We dodged in and out of the crowds, weaving our way to the back of the fairgrounds, where the food trucks had parked. Tom Sawyer's cheery yellow trailer stood out like a canary in a coal mine. We waltzed right past the line at the counter and knocked on the window. Already swamped with orders, Leon gave us a quick wave. He twisted his cap around backward and shouted something over his shoulder. Through the glass, I could see Daddy working the fry basket. The smell of catfish and hush puppies frying golden-crisp made my mouth water something fierce.

"These people won't know what hit them with fish this good."

AC nodded, already holding her stomach.

"Eye on the prize, AC. You can do this. Breathe through your mouth, not your nose." I inhaled a big, showy breath of air through my mouth and then let it out real slow. "You can soak up all the Miss Catfish pageantry you want in two hours."

AC gave me the stink eye. "You mean one."

"Right."

"Hi!" Mrs. Willoughby waved us around to the back of the truck. "You gals, come around here, and I'll fetch you some aprons real quick."

I looked at AC. "How can she be so nice to us, seeing that we burned down her chicken coop?"

AC opened her mouth to reply, but the door flew open.

"Here you go!" Mrs. W shook out two linen aprons stamped with the Tom Sawyer's Catfish Hole logo. "Now just slip them over your neck, like so, and tie them in the back. You got it." She beamed at us like a proud grandma, making me feel worse.

"Thank you, Mrs. Willoughby," AC said.

"Yeah. Thank you," I added.

"You two are more than welcome. I appreciate the good help." She clasped her hands together. "Let's see now, what to do first."

"Uh. Mrs. Willoughby?"

"Yes, Vilonia?"

"I'm really sorry about your henhouse."

"Honey, your daddy and I've talked. It's mighty responsible of you to speak up, and I appreciate and accept your apology." She squeezed my shoulder and winked. "I birthed two boys. I know how they can be. Accidents happen, but they still have consequences."

I nodded. "Yes, ma'am."

"And I trust you've learned a valuable lesson."

"If you mean don't sneak to places I shouldn't, and never trust boys, then consider me taught."

Mrs. Willoughby threw her head back and laughed. "Don't you worry over it anymore. My hens will think they've hit the lottery when their new coop is finished. Now, scoot. We've got orders piling up. One of you can take beans and the other cole-slaw. There's not too much space in there, so if you get hot or claustrophobic, come on out and help these boys clear tables. I've gotta go now. Have mercy, your daddy can fry the best fish this side of the Mississippi."

"Well"—AC turned to me—"I know where I'll be."

I grinned. "You know where to find me, too. If we start now, I'll still have time to hit the game booths."

"And I'll make my call time."

"Deal." With that, I trotted up the metal step into the food truck.

The first hour blew by. Even AC admitted it wasn't all that bad, as she got unlimited sweet tea and free bites of banana pudding. Plus, many customers were either friends of ours or she knew them from Neely's nail salon. I think it helped they wished her well on her performance.

"So you're going to play some games?" AC asked, turning her apron in.

"You know it. But don't worry, I'll be sure to watch my best friend dance." I leaned out the window and blew a strand of hair out of my eyes.

"You'd better. I'm on after the introductions." Her hands flew to the top of her head to check the status of her bun.

"Introductions. Got it."

"Toodles." She spun on her heel and was gone.

"Break a leg!" I shouted, and slid the window closed.

The next hour was hopping but steamy hot inside the truck. I gladly turned my apron in and told Daddy I'd catch him later. Leon, who'd worked half the day, had already run off to find his friends.

I moseyed over to the other side of the park, passing my share of stilt walkers and bubble blowers on the way. Music blared for the Cake Walk. Kids and adults marched around in the circle until the music stopped. Sort of like my heart. Mama had run the Cake Walk for the last three years. But not this year. This year, she couldn't even manage to bake one cake. The Willoughby twins, obviously on break as well, saw me watching and waved as they marched by on the numbered squares. I waved back, and the music stopped. A number, fifteen, was called, and Rory Willoughby's hand shot into the air. His brother punched him in the arm, arguing he'd won instead. Either way, the cake was going home with them.

I turned to go, thinking that any of those cakes would taste like sorrow and sadness compared to Mama's. I'd made it as far as the bouncy castle when someone shouted, "Vilonia!"

Rory caught up to me. His hair hung in waves across his forehead, and his shirt matched his clover-green eyes.

"Nice win on the cake."

He jammed his hands into his pockets. "Thanks. Red velvet."

"Yum. Mama makes one every Christmas. Where's Ransom?" I asked, letting a balloon twister pass between us.

"Trying for the Snickers one. And AC?"

"Backstage. She's dancing after the contestants' introductions. You should watch her."

"How about some games first?"

I smiled.

We each tried a round of ring toss and lost. Then my stomach growled. I'd been so busy working the food truck, I'd forgotten to actually eat. I needed fuel. I couldn't bring my A-game to win a fish if I was light-headed. Luckily, our volunteer wristbands allowed us free snow cones. Rory got watermelon sherbet. I choose tiger's blood, the fiercest flavor I could find.

We polished them off, and a giant voice boomed, "Step right up. Everyone's a winner. Here, you in the green tee, this dog's all yours." A gigantic plush beagle spun over our heads, suspended from the tent by a wire. "All you gotta do is pop one balloon. It's easy. See?"

Rory raised an eyebrow, and I snickered. We stood by and watched as the carnival worker tied off a big pink balloon in his hand and then punctured it with a red dart.

"Too easy." I laughed. I kept my money in my pocket for whichever game had Pete's goldfish. But Rory couldn't pass up the dare.

He was given three darts. Two red, one purple. Rory completely missed his first throw—the red dart fell short of the board altogether.

"Come on, Rory," I teased. "Ransom could do better blindfolded."

His second and third attempts both bounced off balloons. The carnival worker gave him neon sunglasses and a bag of cotton candy as a consolation prize.

As we walked away, he leaned over and said, "Those games are rigged, I promise."

"Ugh! You're probably right." I pointed to another booth's wall of stuffed prizes. Huge plush flowers with happy faces smiled down on us, as if they were in on the cruel joke. *Ha, you'll never win one of us.* The shelves were crammed with medium bears and giant-size bears. Stuffed toy frogs and brightly colored hats next to the biggest plush cats I've ever seen. And then lower, next to the carnival worker, sat the bin of junk toys. Plastic tops, rubber duckies, yo-yos, neon glow necklaces. It was insane. I stepped back to take it all in and noticed the sign overhead. WIN A GOLDFISH! YOU LEAN, YOU LOSE.

161

"Goldfish!" I couldn't believe my luck. I jabbed Rory in the ribs just as a kid in a red cap turned around.

"Yes!" He held up his prize, one Sunkist goldfish.

"'Kay, Tucker, let's go," a bored teen called. And like that, Tucker and his fish disappeared into the crowd.

Watching him go, something clicked inside my head. I'd seen this Tucker kid before. At the mall. He was the boy who threw the tantrum over the tiger cat.

Rory licked cotton candy off his fingertips. "Are you going to play or not?"

I smirked. "Well, if he can win a goldfish, then so can I."

The barker began calling, "One throw for three dollars. Three throws for five. You look like you have a good arm, little lady."

I rolled my eyes and took a step closer.

Rory grabbed my arm and whispered, "Remember these games are rigged."

Sensing he may lose a customer, the barker talked fast. "Knock over all six, and you win a prize."

"I know," I said, under my breath, "but this is the milk bottle pyramid! I throw strikes like you catch hens."

Rory's eyebrow shot up.

I marched up to the counter and pulled a five out of my back pocket. It was all the money I had left.

"Here you go, whenever you're ready." The barker set three ratty softballs in a triangle formation on the counter in front of me. "Be sure to stay behind the table, now. No leaning, and good luck."

I picked up the first ball and placed my fingers over the seams. It felt right, if a bit light, in my hand. Next, I studied the tower of bottles. Three jugs made the bottom, two stood in the middle, and one sat on top.

I aimed for the bottom row. My arm flew back. Then, *whoosh!* The ball slipped from my fingers and bounced into the bottom right corner. The top bottle swayed but didn't topple.

That was a warm-up, Vi. That's why you bought three chances. I rolled my shoulders back and took a deep breath. Ready. Set. Throw!

The ball sailed from my grip, and the top bottle tumbled to the floor.

"Nice!" Rory cheered behind me.

"And she got one!" The worker held the bottle up for all to see. A few cheers followed.

But I didn't let myself celebrate. I had one throw and five bottles left. I took a step back, found my target, and everything else faded away. My arm whipped round. I grunted.

Thunk!

Bull's-eye. The ball struck the middle bottle on the bottom row. The bottles toppled in four different directions.

"Yes!" I jumped up in the air. Rory and I high-fived.

"And we have a winner!" the barker announced. "Name your prize, any prize." He motioned to the rows of plush toys.

"Actually, I want a goldfish."

"Ah, you snooze, you lose. The last one just disappeared. They've been the hottest prize today."

"What?" I shook my head, trying to understand.

"We don't have any more. That kid won the last one."

"Will you be getting any more?" Rory asked.

"Afraid not. Pick a prize, would ya?" he ordered as he restacked the tower for the next player.

But I was too shocked and upset to choose anything else. I wanted a fish.

"Sometime before Christmas would be nice," said the teenager in line behind me.

"Fine," I huffed, looking at my options. Then it hit me. "The big orange cat, please."

"Garfield?" Rory asked. "I didn't know you liked him."

"I don't. But I may know someone who does."

Chapter Twenty-Three

With no time to explain, I darted into the crowd, looking for a boy in a red cap. "Excuse me." "Pardon me." "So sorry."

"Hey, watch it!"

"Sorry, Mister, uh, Coach Harriman," I called over my shoulder to my old softball coach.

"Hey, Speed Racer," Rory said, catching up to me, "isn't the fancy Miss Catfish stage that way? I think I see Ransom and Leon grabbing seats."

"Yeah, but they haven't started yet. You go ahead."

"Oof. Excuse me." Rory dodged a mother pushing a double stroller, then strode back to me. "You do know your best friend is about to take the stage."

"Yes," I huffed. Clearly, I was not the track star of the family. "But I've got to catch that kid. Save me a seat!" And I sprinted away from the stage, leaving Rory standing still in the pulsating crowd, just as a magician turned some colorful scarves into doves. The audience cheered. My lungs burned and my feet slapped the pavement. Up ahead, a red cap dashed around a corner.

I bolted forward.

Tucker stopped at last. Out of breath, I jogged up to him as he showed his fish to the bored teenager, maybe his older sister? Or babysitter? Whoever she was, she wore cut-off shorts and braces across her teeth. It sure wasn't his mom from the mall.

"Hi." I explained my dilemma to her and asked if I could speak with Tucker about his prize. She shrugged in an *up to you* kind of way.

I bent down. "Hi, Tucker. My name is Vilonia. I really, *really* need a fish for an important school assignment. I was wondering if you'd want to trade that boring fish, that you can't take too many places, for this gigantic fluffy cat that, when you use your imagination, kind of looks like a tiger!" I made my hand into a claw and fake roared.

Tucker tilted his head to the side and squinted. I could see the little wheels turning in his brain while he sized up Garfield with a scowl. He held his fish in front of his nose and then dropped his arm back to his side.

My heart sank.

"It's your choice, Tuck," his babysitter said.

I smiled at him, hoping I looked kind and patient and not desperate.

"Okay." Tucker held out his bag. "You can have him."

I wanted to hug him, but I gave him Garfield instead. "Thank you so much! I know you'll take great care of this, er, tiger cat. His name's Garfield."

Tucker's eyes grew wide. He looked at Garfield and smiled. "Okay."

"Okay." I smiled too, and held onto my precious plastic bag with a death grip.

"Okay!" the babysitter agreed.

"Bye, Tucker." I waved. "I've got to go now." And I turned on my heel and ran straight into Mr. Reyes.

"Whoa!" He struggled to balance one of Guy's famous shakes and a paper plate carrying the biggest funnel cake known to man. "We almost had a caketastrophe." So during spring break Mr. Reyes paired his Captain America tee with a *Boston Strong* cap.

"Oh, um. Hi, Mr. Reyes," I said, quickly hiding the goldfish underneath my raincoat. Thank goodness I had listened to Daddy and brought it. "I like your cap."

"Thank you, Vilonia. Are you having a good break?"

"Yep." I smiled. "A *great* break." *Please don't ask about Max. Please don't ask about Max.*

"Well, that is great to hear." Mr. Reyes's eyebrows creased. Could he tell I was acting strange? "How's Max?"

"Max. Max is . . . um? Max is good." I beamed. "A little lonely. I think he misses you." My cheeks grew hot. I was a horrible liar, and Mr. Reyes was no dummy. But I don't think he saw the goldfish underneath my raincoat.

"Well, it's a good thing I'll see him the day after tomorrow!" He winked.

I started to respond, but the crowd by the stage went bananas. Out stepped the master of ceremonies, our local radio DJ, Richie Rhapsody. "The forty-seventh annual Miss Catfish Pageant will begin shortly. So y'all buy yourself a cold drink, grab a seat, and get ready to see some of Howard County's brightest, most talented stars."

"We love you, Richie!" screamed a fan.

"I love you, too," he replied.

"Nice seeing you, Mr. Reyes, but I've got to find a seat." I raised my voice over the whistling crowd.

"And I'd better get this cake delivered while it's still warm."

"Oh, sure." I stepped aside and watched Mr. Reyes and his *Boston Strong* cap walk away.

The sun hung low in the sky now. The string of lights shone zigzag across walkways, connecting booths like twinkling laces on a tennis shoe. I pulled the new goldfish back out of hiding.

Music filtered through the loudspeakers. The first group of contestants paraded across the stage, single file. All I knew was I didn't give a hoot about the new Miss Catfish. All I cared about was seeing Ray Charles. Make that *adopting* Ray Charles.

Please let him be here.

Richie Rhapsody's announcer voice filled the late afternoon air, but I couldn't tell you a single thing he said. Let alone what color the girls' dresses were. Or what song the band played. My heart beat to one drum, *Ray Charles. Ray Charles. Ray Charles.*

I made a bet with myself I could find his booth before AC took the stage. I took a left, and a long alleyway of vendors opened before me, but halfway down I spotted a paw-printed logo. The Animal Shelter's logo. I rushed over.

A gaggle of kids crowded around a portable pen. I wedged my shoulder in between two boys. Six yellow Lab puppies tumbled and nipped at one another, chasing tennis balls and chewing on rawhides, blissfully unaware of the attention they were receiving. Except for one, who'd stuck his nose through the grate, licking a preschooler's fingers. The little girl giggled and shrieked, surprised by the tickles.

"Mona, come stand by Daddy and me, please." A round lady, talking to one of the shelter workers, snapped her fingers to get Mona's attention. But Mona shrieked, fixated on the pups.

They were cute all right, but they weren't Ray Charles. I turned to the main table, where Mona's parents stood, and I wondered what I'd say when I got up there. *So, did you bring Ray Charles? I'm the one who called about him last night.*

And the next thing I knew, there were nods and thank-yous, and Mona's dad, bald and every bit as round as Mona's mom, shook the volunteer's hand while slipping some brochures into his shirt pocket. They turned to leave and left me smiling and looking stunned at the tanned shelter worker with huge hair, shimmery lips, and paw-print earrings.

"Miss Sogbottom?"

"Hey there, Vilonia. What can I do for you?"

"I—uh," I stammered, and replayed the phone call in my mind. I knew the volunteer's voice had sounded familiar. Why hadn't I put the two together?

"I see you've won yourself a new fish. Today must be your lucky day!" Miss Sogbottom smiled and took a long sip of her Guy's milkshake. Going by the Nilla wafer on top, my guess was banana cream.

"Hi." I cleared my throat. "I called last night, about Ray—I mean Izzy. Is he here?"

Miss Sogbottom's cheerleader smile slipped faster than a meteorite falling to earth.

"Oh, honey. That was you?"

I nodded. "Is he all right?"

"Oh, yes, he's fine, but . . . I'm so sorry, Vilonia. Izzy's spoken for."

Spoken for? What did that even mean?

"Excuse me?" I whispered, taking a step back.

"Well, um. Someone dropped off an application at the shelter a little bit ago, along with the adoption fee. But don't you worry. I'm sure *everything* will shake out just fine."

Shake out just fine? What? We're talking about actual *lives* here—mine and Mama's and Ray Charles's. My brain stopped processing her words. My heart splintered into a million tiny shards, and a crater-size void took its place.

"Vilonia. Are you all right?" It was Mr. Reyes, with his half-eaten funnel cake.

I pulled the new goldfish to my chest and blinked. "I—I've got to go."

Chapter Twenty-Four

So much for Miss Sogbottom's promise of matching Izzy/Ray Charles to the best home. *Mine.*

Hot, angry tears blurred my vision, but I knew one thing. I had to get out of there, and the fish was coming with me. I stumbled a few steps toward the packed staging area. Miss Bettina stood three yards in front of me, in floral pant-suit glory, talking into a microphone. I ducked the other way, underneath a couple holding hands.

I pushed through the dense crowd. My jacket caught on one of those temporary fences, and I tugged hard to break free. Jazzy music drifted through the air from one of two tall speakers as girls in shimmery gowns paraded offstage. I'd missed the introductions. I craned my neck to get a glimpse of AC waiting in the wings backstage, practicing her deep breaths before she went on, but I couldn't see a thing. Oh well. Nothing mattered now. Daddy said he wouldn't let me get a dog, and now The Universe agreed.

I put my head down. The music changed tempo, and a gap formed in the crowd. I broke away, sprinting like the wind, as my best friend since forever fluttered like an exotic butterfly to center stage. I ran past stage left, where Neely's sky-high updo caught the corner of my eye. No doubt some—okay, all—of the pageant contestants were her clients. I blew past the carnival games and their obnoxious barkers, past the Cake Walk, past the Himalayan, the Maze of Mirrors. Past all the boys taking advantage of the now-empty lines.

My legs pumped faster. *And Leon does this for fun,* I thought as I exited through the gate. By the time I reached the nearest sidewalk, my side began to cramp. I slowed to a walk. The run had done me good; it felt good to use my muscles, to burn off some anger. Kind of like throwing strikes.

I kept on, one foot in front of the other. There was only one place I wanted to be. The sky had grown darker, even though the sun hadn't set. A drop of water fell on my cheek. Then another on my arm. I reached for my raincoat, and the sky opened wide. Rain pelted the sidewalk, the trees, and me, but my navy raincoat with green frogs was gone. I spun around, but it was nowhere to be found. Four whole weeks, that's how long I'd kept it. I sprinted the rest of the way home. By the time I reached our house, I was wetter than an otter. Mama would be so mad. I pushed on the front door, but it was locked tight.

"Mama! You home?" I rang the bell.

No answer. But all the lights were on. Weird. I wrapped my arms around my middle and studied the row of empty drives and hazy porch lights. My whole street was at the festival.

I shivered and walked around back. That door was locked too, and the spare key underneath the planter was gone.

"Come on," I whispered, trying to open the door to Daddy's shop. "Just open."

But it was bolted tight. I rested my head against the door. Cold and exhausted, I held up the carnival fish. Drops of water pinged off the plastic bubble. He (she?) stared at me, Miss Responsible. "Well, I know of one more place."

The rope ladder was slippery wet. I climbed onto the first rung, and seeing I needed both hands, I pinched the top of New Max's bag between my teeth. Up and up we climbed. Until my head met the trapdoor.

I hoisted myself up into the tree house and shut the window to keep out the rain. I shivered. I was cold, wet, and sad. My chest felt too small for the crater in my heart. Was this how Mama's sadness felt? I turned on the magical twinkle lights. The row of candy beckoned, but all the licorice in the world couldn't make me feel better. I couldn't look at the picture of Nana on the wall. Or of my family. Instead, I slunk to the floor in a puddle, cradling Mr. Reyes's new library fish in my lap.

So this is what happens when you try to be responsible, I thought. You kill one fish, win another, and the dog you have your heart set on is stolen right out from under you. I had worked so hard, had written so many obituaries. I broke down and sobbed. Tears slipped off my face onto the fish's plastic case. I'm sure he didn't know what to think of his new owner.

I have no idea how long we sat there like that, the two of us, while the wind whipped, the rain beat, and the leaves shivered and shook around us outside.

Car doors slammed. I peeked through the shutters and saw headlights cut off in my drive. My heart leapt. Suddenly, there was nowhere I'd rather be than with my family.

"Come on, fish. Let's go." I threw the trapdoor back and half slipped, half slid down the ladder, almost forgetting to pull the trapdoor shut.

Another car pulled into the drive. And then voices, shouting. I ran across the yard, splashing in mud puddles, swinging the bag with the fish.

First I saw Mama and Daddy run into the house. And then Neely drove up in her pink sedan, hopped the curb, and slammed on her brakes. Out tumbled AC in her twirly blue costume, looking like a wet snowflake. And then Mr. Reyes and Miss Sogbottom climbed out of the back. What in the world?

"AC! Over here! Mr. Reyes!" But the rain drowned my voice.

I ran up onto the porch and pushed open the door, never in my life so happy to walk into the warmth of my own house.

"Vilonia!" Mama wrapped me up with a bear hug. "We were so worried about you, baby. You weren't by the Ferris wheel. You missed Ava Claire's dance . . ." I glanced at AC, who looked down at her toes. "*Then* Miss Sogbottom found us and said you ran off, upset."

"Tadpole! You're home." Daddy picked me up and gave me a twirl. "I've caught a fish drier than you. Where is your raincoat?"

"Sorry, Daddy. I lost it at the festival." I pushed strands of wet hair out of my face.

"Next time tell someone before you take off, you hear? Better yet, take someone with you."

I nodded. They still hadn't noticed the fish.

"I sent Leon home to check on you, but he ran back saying you weren't here—"

"We were starting to get scared," Mama interrupted.

"But I was here. I was up in the—"

Leon and a small army of soggy boys burst through the door, their sneakers squeaking across the floor. "We looked everywhere, Dad," Leon gasped, then spotted me. "Oh, hey."

"You're home!" Ransom and Rory chimed the obvious.

"Here," Leon said, "I found this by the stage. You owe me." He held out my navy raincoat with the tiny green frogs and winked. I think he was teasing. Maybe.

"You kids will catch cold unless we get you properly warmed up. Terry, you grab the sweaters, and I'll put on some tea. Vilonia has some serious explaining to do." Mama headed for the kitchen, and my stomach clinched.

Beagles. I didn't want to explain anything. Mama spun back around. "Vi, you run upstairs and change first. Give me that fish, so I can put it in a bowl."

"Yes, ma'am."

"And Ava Claire, why don't you borrow a pair of Vilonia's pajamas. I'll hang your costume up to dry."

"Thank you, Mrs. B."

Mama hustled out of the room.

"Looks like your mama's back," AC mumbled as we climbed the stairs.

I remembered what Daddy had said one week ago, right before I hopped on my bike and rescued Eleanor from a certain and horrible death: *Every day is different when it comes to Mama.*

I opened my door, still flashing the KEEP OUT!!! sign made before Max's memorial, and sighed. "I really hope you're right," I said, and switched on the light.

AC leaned against the doorjamb with her arms crossed and her mouth stretched into a thin, tight line. "*She* saw me dance."

I tugged open my dresser and froze.

AC's face flushed, and her hands flew through the air as she spoke. "Do you have *any* idea how it feels to have your best friend skip the *biggest* dance of your *career*?"

"AC, I'm—"

"No, you wouldn't. Because *I've* been there for you. I worked the food truck, even though I hate fish. And!" she sputtered, waving her hands at all of the dog posters plastered on my wall. "You've been *so* obsessed with this precious pet campaign of yours that *you* don't even care about anyone other than Ray Charles!" AC's voice shook, and I knew from experience she was near tears. "Really, Vilonia? Best friends don't—"

"STOP it. Just stop!" I sank onto my bed and buried my face in my hands. "You *knew* the Great Pet Campaign was bigger than me and Ray Charles." My voice became a whisper. "It was about helping Mama get better after my nana *died*, remember?"

AC didn't speak.

I took a shaky breath and studied the colorful threads woven into my rug. I wanted all of this to be over, to go away. I wanted things to return to when Nana was still with us. Then AC and I would be fine, and Mama would be happy. Happy writing. Happy cooking. Happy driving Leon and I around town. But going back wasn't an option.

Moving forward was.

"Listen," I said with a sniffle. "I'm sorry I didn't watch your dance. I know it was important to you. I messed up. I told you I'd be there, then I wasn't."

Ava Claire crossed her arms, and I continued, "There will be other dogs, though none as perfect as Ray Charles." I gave her an uncertain smile. "But there's only one you. I hope you'll still be my friend."

Ava Claire sat down beside me.

"Friend for life." She hugged me. Her sequins poked into my skin, and I imagined hugging a porcupine. "We will find another dog. And you weren't the only one missing tonight," she added, rubbing the goose bumps away on her arms.

I frowned and walked back to my dresser. "The general?"

"Yep." She slipped out of her wet tutu.

"You know, like I do, he would have done anything to see you dance." I dug through my drawers and pulled out two sets of pajamas.

"Well, anything wasn't enough." Her chin quivered, from either disappointment or the cold, or a bit of both. "But maybe he can see me in two weeks."

I handed her my striped pajamas and kept the mismatched set for myself. "What's in two weeks?"

"Since the pageant was called due to weather, the director said they'd likely reschedule. It's the first time in festival history we didn't crown a queen." She held up the pajama top to make sure it'd fit. "The Yankees, really?"

"What? They're the warmest ones I have." I poked my head through my clean shirt.

"I'm sorry I got mad. If only I'd known when I didn't see you in the audience that I wouldn't even finish my dance." She giggled. "You should have heard the contestants squeal when their hair and makeup got wet."

I laughed. "You do look like a droopy dewdrop."

She smirked. "I was going for soggy snowflake."

By the time we came back downstairs, the tea was ready and butterflies had assembled in my stomach. The company had grown by one (that Miss Bettina, always after the scoop), and everyone had gathered around to hear about my night. *Great.*

Leon perched himself on the sofa next to his soon-to-be teammates, who had, from the looks of it, raided Daddy's closet for old sweatshirts and scarfed down a box of Little Debbies like it was their last meal on earth, not a post-race snack. Normally I'd be annoyed they ate them all, but I was too nervous at the moment to eat.

Mama handed me a warm mug while I tried to get comfy in my favorite chair. Behind me, Neely and Miss Bettina debated whether acrylic nails or Shellac lasted the longest. Across the room, on the piano bench, Mr. Reyes whispered something that made Miss Sogbottom laugh. Are they *flirting*? I glanced at AC, who confirmed my hunch by wriggling her eyebrows behind her own steaming mug.

"Okay, Tadpole," Daddy began, "now that you're settled, why don't you tell us why you ran off and about gave your mama here a heart attack." He hooked a protective arm around her waist.

"Yes, inquiring minds want to know." Mama sipped her tea.

I drew a big breath. "Pugs."

"Pugs?" Mama asked.

"It's complicated." I looked at Nana's portrait hanging by the piano and remembered her words. *You're a fighter, Vi. You can do this.* So I gripped my tea with trembling fingers and asked, "Where should I start?"

"Start at the beginning, hon. It's usually the best place." Miss Bettina gave my shoulder a reassuring squeeze.

"Start from your heart," Mama said.

So I did. I started at the beginning, from my heart. I covered Nana's passing, Mama's Infinite Sadness, and how rescuing Eleanor Roostevelt had led me to the FEELING BLUE? poster at the vet. Which in turn fueled the Great Pet Campaign even more, because dog ownership eases most any heartache. If that's not in *Winn-Dixie*, it should be.

"Mama and Daddy, I'm sorry I ran. I know we had a plan to meet, but when I got to the shelter's booth, and Miss Sogbottom told me the dog I'd seen was no longer available, I felt so sad I bolted."

Tears ran down Mama's cheeks. Miss Bettina passed her a box of tissues and then plucked one for herself.

"I can't believe you planned all of this to help me." Mama dabbed at her eyes.

"Oh, there's more," I told her.

And by the time our tea was either gone or cold, I'd spilled everything. Tea and sympathy does that to a person, so Nana said.

I spilled how I'd tried to be responsible. I'd done laundry

and dishes and had written obits for Mama so she'd stay gainfully employed. (I paused a second for Mama to blow her nose.) I talked about how I'd brought Max home to prove just how responsible I was, and then I choked up when I talked about losing him. Mr. Reyes smiled. I longed to ask him about the rumor, which number Max my Max really was, but decided to save that question for another rainy day. Of course I said I'd wanted to give Max the most memorable send-off ever, never dreaming I'd burn down my friends' henhouse. I told of catching chickens after dark on a rooftop and how hard I'd worked at the food truck and then afterward to win Mr. Reyes a new fish. And then I glanced over at Miss Sogbottom and plumb lost it.

Mama came over and squeezed my hand. "We knew you wanted a dog. We just didn't know the length you were willing to go to get one."

"I haven't heard a story this heartwarming since . . ." Miss Bettina pulled a pad of paper from her handbag and began jotting notes. "Do you have any cookies?"

Then it was Mama's turn to spill. Remember how I'd found that folder in the pantry next to the Little Debbies? It turned out Mama had seen Miss Bettina's e-mail about the Lafferty obituary. In fact, that's why she was working on the porch. She had just sat down with her computer when a message appeared thanking her for a job well done. Never mind Mama hadn't written a single word. After a few e-mails and one awkward phone call to the paper, Mama knew someone had been writing obits on her behalf. . . .

"So when Miss Bettina mentioned my new obits had more punch and personality, and I knew *I* hadn't written anything in ages, I got suspicious." Mama's eyebrow arched, and she motioned with her teacup to her boss.

"Your mama wanted to know who was writing them, then, if not me," Miss Bettina added. "We couldn't imagine who else could write with such zest. Subscribers have flooded our in-boxes with compliments."

Mama set her cup down and nodded. "That's when she reminded me she'd been leaving the materials with you, my capable almost-ten-year-old, and everything snapped into place."

"Aha! I knew it." Leon bolted upright on the sofa. "I knew you'd been sneaking Mom's computer."

"I'd never been prouder of you or so mad at myself," Daddy spoke up. "I could hardly believe it when your mama called to tell me. I should have noticed you were juggling too much, but I didn't. Instead, I harped on the few things that fell through the cracks. You've done good, Tadpole."

Mama nodded. "So, Vilonia baby, yes, you're a handful, but you've also held this family together in more ways than one." Mama's voice broke. She paused a moment to collect herself, then said, "Daddy and I have talked."

I swallowed. Usually when they talked about me, it spelled T-R-O-U-B-L-E.

Mama smiled. "Vilonia, your daddy and I have watched you take care of skunks, hens, and a fish. And in light of recent events—"

"Yes?" I winced.

"We agree that you are the most responsible fourth grader we know. And if anyone deserves a dog, you do."

"Really?" I jumped up. It was a good thing my teacup was near empty, or I'd have sloshed it all over Miss Bettina's pants.

Daddy grinned as big as day and wrapped his arm around Mama. "Your mama here drove to the shelter and paid the adoption fee this afternoon."

I gasped. "That was you?"

Mama nodded. "I had a little help." She pointed to Miss Sogbottom, who leaned forward in her seat like she was about to share a big, fat secret. "I'm sorry I couldn't tell you at the festival, Vilonia. I didn't want to spoil the surprise."

"Surprise?" I clasped my hands together in front of my chest to contain my leaping heart. "Do you mean Ray Charles is going to be mine?"

Mama and Daddy exchanged looks. "Now, sweetie," Mama began, "I don't know who Ray Charles is, but Miss Sogbottom showed me the sweetest pup named Izzy who has the cutest little sweetheart nose . . ."

"Hold on," I said, and flew up the stairs to HQ. I grabbed my very own copy of *Winn-Dixie* and returned to the living room, waving the flyer that'd doubled as a bookmark. "You mean him?"

Now Mama gasped. "Why . . . that's him all right. Where in the world did you get this?"

"It IS Ray Charles! I knew it." I jumped up and tackle-hugged them both. "Thank you, thank you, thank you! This is better than cake." Happy tears brimmed in my eyes. "Can I see him?"

Daddy scratched his beard and looked to Miss Sogbottom. "Hazel, what's the timeline on that?"

Miss Sogbottom cleared her throat. "Well. You're welcome to visit first thing tomorrow. We need to observe you interacting with the puppy before we can make it official, though I don't anticipate any trouble."

"Trouble from me? Never." The whole room laughed.

"Well, I guess we Beebes got a dog," Daddy said, putting his arm around me and raising his other in a toast. "To Vilonia and Ray Charles."

"To Vilonia," said Mr. Reyes.

"To Vilonia," said Miss Sogbottom and Miss Bettina.

"To Vilonia," echoed Neely and AC and the entire middle-school track team, counting Leon, who rolled his eyes so high they about stuck.

"To family," said Mama. "But first, how did you choose the name Ray Charles?"

"Easy," I said, lifting my teacup high. "Nana."

Chapter Twenty-Five

The next day was Sunday, and I could hardly wait for church to let out. Not because I was anticipating Daddy's tacos, which were kiss-the-cook delicious. I was anxiously waiting for the Animal Shelter to open. But first I promised Ava Claire celebratory manicures at Neely's salon.

Mama dropped me off at the door. She couldn't stay, as she had to get home and bake a sour cream pound cake to drop by the newspaper, her way of thanking Miss Bettina for tolerating my shenanigans and for giving her an extra two weeks to ease back into work. I told her to not push herself too hard. She promised she wouldn't and would sneak in a nap while the cake cooled. Maybe her new medicine was helping.

"Make a sign warning Leon to keep his grubby mitts off," I said through the car window.

"Oh, don't you worry. I may not have baked in a while, but I haven't forgotten how to post mild threats." She gripped the gearshift to move the car into reverse, then stopped. "Your daddy will be by soon to pick you up. Love you, Vi."

"I love you, too, Mama."

I waved, and the minivan sped away.

Inside, Neely and Ava Claire were all ready for me.

"Welcome, Vilonia! My next client won't be here for half an hour, so you girls are free to play. I've got to go to the back and straighten some inventory."

"Sure. Thanks, Mrs. Nutter."

Ava Claire waved me over to the wall of nail polish. "Pick out a polish."

I wrinkled my nose. "Who knew there were one zillion shades of red? I'm not so sure about this."

AC laughed. "I guess it can be overwhelming. Neely did buy these new decals. You should take a look."

"Maybe so." I flipped through the sheets of stickers. Every color, print, or pattern imaginable had been shrunk, turned into tiny stickers, and then sold as "nail art." There were zebra stripes, checks, flags, butterflies, flowers, letters, sports themes, and even one sheet with decals of bitty glazed donuts. In the end, I chose the paw prints.

Not that I ever doubted her, but AC can give a mean manicure. My nails had never looked so shiny in their almost ten years. I had just finished telling her that Mama was going home to bake a pound cake, when the door chimed.

"Neely! Your next appointment is here," AC called to the back of the salon without looking up. "I have to clean up this dab of polish . . . right here." She rolled my pinky to the side and squeezed a little tighter.

I glanced up at the waiting client and blinked. Twice. His desert fatigues and army cap seemed out of place in a funky nail salon. He winked at me as he set his duffel down like it was made of air.

My jaw dropped.

"Yeah. I was wondering where I could get a decent pedicure. These boots are killing my—"

"Dad!" AC flew out of her seat, smudging my pinky paw print, but what did I care? The general was home! I ran over and flung my arms around them both. Hearing commotion, Neely hustled to the front, screamed with joy, and burst into happy tears. I slipped away, unnoticed, out the back door. They needed to enjoy their moment as a family.

AC had waited a long time for General Nutter to come home. Almost as long as I'd been hoping for a dog, and that's saying something. I sprinted around the building to the bench out front, where I parked my backside and waited for my own daddy with a song in my heart. That's the thing with hope: If you keep hoping long enough, and hard enough, even with life's disappointments, something good will happen. Today was proof.

"Vilonia, you sitting here drumming your fingers on the side of the car isn't going to make the time tick away any faster."

"I know." I sighed. "I can't wait to see him!"

Daddy smiled. "Same here, kiddo. Same here."

We heard the jangle of keys, and the door opened. Miss Sogbottom's cheery face appeared, and she waved us in. She must have come from church as well. Her heels click-clacked across the tile floor.

"I usually volunteer on Saturdays, but since I know your family so well, I told my boss I'd come in this afternoon." She leaned over to me and whispered, "Anyway, I wanted to see Ray Charles again for myself. I think he's even stronger."

"I bet." My eyes shone. "He's a fighter. I knew the moment I saw him."

She led us around the counter to the back of the office, where the kennels were. An older dog, a shepherd of some sort, barked once. There were a few kennels with cats. One dachshund with floppy ears looked at us and then closed his eyes.

It didn't take but a few seconds for me to find Ray Charles. He was snoozing and adorable. I let out a tiny squeal. He opened his eyes, stretched his front legs, and yawned.

"He's so cute."

"He really is," said Daddy.

"Would you like to hold him?" Miss Sogbottom asked, unlocking his door.

"May I?"

She laughed, flashing rows of beautiful teeth. "He's yours!"

189

She picked him up, still groggy, and placed him into my arms. He felt as warm and fuzzy as a fleece blanket. My heart about burst from happiness. Then a line from *Winn-Dixie* popped into my head. *And all of a sudden, I felt happy. I had a dog. I had a job. I had Miss Franny Block for a friend.* Yep. India Opal and I weren't too far off. I now had a dog. I'd had a job. And I counted AC, the Willoughbys, and Miss Sogbottom as friends.

I held Ray Charles as long as I could, planting a little kiss on his forehead when I had to put him back. Since he was a newborn, he had to stay five more weeks until he was ready to come home.

"I hate to leave him," I said, handing him back to Miss Sogbottom.

"I know, but we'll take great care of him and get him ready to come home soon." She smiled. "And you are welcome to visit any time you wish."

"I'll bring some of Mama's cake." I stood on my tiptoes and whispered into her ear, "I still owe you for Max."

Miss Sogbottom grinned. "You're on."

"Well, get ready," I said. "Because I'll be by every day."

"She means it too," Daddy added.

"That's not a problem." Miss Sogbottom laughed again. "We'll see you soon, Vilonia."

"You better believe it!"

• • •

I could smell Mama's sour cream pound cake cooling on the windowsill before we'd reached our door.

"Boy howdy, did I miss your mama's baking." Daddy rubbed his belly and breathed in whiffs of vanilla and cinnamon.

"You and me both. And lucky for us, Mama baked *two* cakes." I pointed to the sticky note on the counter specifying which cake was "ours" and which was "do not touch, or else."

I knew Mama missed being in the kitchen too. It was her happy place, after all, and it'd been too many days (fifty-one, to be exact) since Mama had been really and truly happy.

Boy howdy, had I missed *her*. Period. Together, we cooked dinner in Nana's cast-iron skillet—grilled cheeses slathered with mayo—while jazz music played over the radio. I scrubbed dishes afterward just so we could visit, and it didn't even seem like a chore. We talked about all the things we loved, and missed, about Nana. Mama told me how living with the Infinite Sadness was plain exhausting, how she didn't even feel like herself, and I filled her in on the general's homecoming and how his combat boots were killing his feet. She set her dish towel down, mid-dry. Looking over at me, all misty-eyed, she whispered, "You know, Vilonia? I'll always miss Nana, that won't change, no matter how much time marches on. I still feel lost without her, but maybe I'm finding my way home too."

"Welcome home, Mama." I hugged her waist. "We're glad you're back."

"Me too, baby. Me too."

For helping with the dishes, Mama let me cut myself a thick slice of "our" cake. I wrapped my piece up in a napkin and headed upstairs to HQ with pound cake in one hand and Mama's laptop under my arm. New Max did a flip turn in his bowl, while I scarfed down my slice. I tried to savor it, as it'd been two months since I'd had cake from Janet Beebe's oven, but in the end, I ate it in three bites.

"New Max, you don't know what you're missing by eating fish flakes."

He swam to the side of the bowl and waited.

"We go back to school tomorrow, New Max. You'll love Howard County Elementary and the library. Mr. Reyes is the best librarian in the world." I tossed New Max a piece of food. "Well, good night, sleep tight. I have one last thing to do."

I powered up Mama's laptop right as a *knock, knock* sounded at my door. Mama poked her head in. "Forgot your milk." She set it on my nightstand and peeked at my computer screen.

"You feeling brave today, Mama?" I scooted over to make room on my bed.

Mama smiled and blinked away a tear. "We're fighters, aren't we? Let's do this."

> To: bettina@howardcountypress.com
> From: janet@howardcountypress.com
> Subject: Lola Mae Dorothy

Lola Mae Dorothy of Howard County, MS, our beloved mother and nana, went to be with her Lord and Savior on Friday, March 4, while shopping for metronomes. She was 68 years young.

Lola Mae was born to Forrest and Alice Susan Copeland on November 18, 1946, in Jackson, MS. The family moved to Fayetteville, AR, before Lola could hold a No. 2 pencil.

Lola Mae attended Root Elementary and Fayetteville High School. She majored in music education at the University of Arkansas, where she met the love of her life, an engineering student named Leroy Dorothy. Legend has it that in a hurry, Leroy entered the wrong auditorium for a lecture, heard Lola practicing a concerto, and proposed marriage. She turned him down. Eventually, the two did marry and stayed married more than forty years.

Lola Mae taught piano students from her home studio in Howard County and loved every minute of it, minus that one prank with a rubber snake.

A longtime member of Third Baptist Church, she also volunteered at a local soup kitchen, where she cooked chicken and dumplings and made her famous banana pudding from scratch, once without the bananas. She called it "banana-less pudding." To be sure, Lola Mae's swift smile and generous scoops warmed as many hearts as stomachs.

Lola Mae is survived by her loving daughter and son-in-law, Janet and Terry Beebe, and her two adoring grandchildren, Leon and Vilonia Beebe, and many friends.

The family wishes to thank all of those who showered them with care and concern the last three months. Donations can be made in Lola's memory to the Lola Mae Dorothy Piano Scholarship Fund in care of the University of Arkansas Music Department.

Arrangements were provided by the Howard County Funeral Home.

Over and out.

Amen.

Janet Beebe's Award-Winning
Sour Cream Pound Cake

"Best served with my world-famous, and now stem-less,
strawberry-infused tea. Please ask a grown-up for help."
—*Vilonia*

2 cups sugar

2 sticks butter

3 eggs, thanks to Eleanor

1 tsp vanilla

1 tsp baking powder

¼ tsp salt

2 cups flour

1 cup sour cream

1 cup fresh or frozen blueberries (optional)

Cinnamon-sugar mixture:

¼ cup brown sugar

1 tsp ground cinnamon

1 cup chopped pecans (optional)

Cream sugar and butter in a large mixing bowl. Add eggs, one at a time, and beat well. Add in the dry ingredients, sour cream, and blueberries, if using. Pour one-half of the batter into a greased and floured Bundt pan and sprinkle one-half of the cinnamon-sugar mixture on top. Pour the remaining batter into the pan followed by the remaining cinnamon-sugar mixture. Bake at 350 degrees Fahrenheit for one hour, an eternity when it comes to cake, but we promise it's worth the wait.

Acknowledgments

Though writing is a solitary endeavor, it takes many people, and cookies, to make a book. My sincerest thanks to the following individuals who helped bring Vilonia to print:

To my intrepid, no-nonsense agent, Caryn Wiseman, who took a chance on me after seeing only a handful of pages. Your wit and wisdom pushed me to the finish line. I'll forever be grateful Big Sur brought us together.

To my editor, the savvy Sylvie Frank, who asked the best questions, tolerated my bouts of indecision, and laughed at the right parts. You deserve a whole cake.

To the entire team at Paula Wiseman Books: Krista Vossen, Katrina Groover, Chava Wolin, Sarah Jane Abbott, and Paula Wiseman. Thank you is not enough. I'm treating you all to Guy's milkshakes. And to Emma Trithart, who so perfectly illustrated Vilonia's personality and spunk. Thank you.

To my friends at Arkansas SCBWI. Your notes made for a better book.

To my critique mates turned close friends, who read Vilonia's story at every stage. The Book Nerds: Karen Akins, Kimberly Loth, and Mandy Silberstein. I love you all.

To Stefanie Wass, fellow dog lover and the best beta reader, and to my debut author group, the Swanky Seventeens, for countless laughs and pep talks.

To Dr. Stacy Furlow and Dr. Paige Partridge for their support and help in answering my medical questions.

To my parents, Mickey and Phillis, who raised two readers. Thank you for turning my lamp off all of those nights I fell asleep reading. And to my twin brother, Ryan. We've come a long way from two-pound preemies. I still call the front seat.

And to Jackson, Zachary, Nathan, Copeland, and Madeleine—my fiercest cheerleaders. I'm your biggest fan and am so lucky you're mine.

And to Jesse, who told me to "write the book already." I love you times infinity.

And thanks always to God for seeing fit to let me live despite my rocky start so I could share these words with you.